MALPERTUIS

STORY OF AN EXTRAORDINARY HOUSE

JEAN RAY

TRANSLATED BY IAIN WHITE

EDITED BY SCOTT NICOLAY

WAKEFIELD PRESS

CAMBRIDGE, MASSACHUSETTS

Wakefield Press, P.O. Box 425645, Cambridge, MA 02142

Originally published as *Malpertuis: Histoire d'une maison fantastique* in 1943.
Published by special arrangement with Alma Éditeur in conjunction with their
duly appointed agent 2 Seas Literary Agency.
© Héritier Jean Ray, 2017 et Alma éditeur, Paris, 2017

Cover image: Clip # 18088, *Barbe Bleu* from the Turconi collection at the
George Eastman Museum.

This book was set in Garamond Premier Pro and Helvetica Neue Pro by Wakefield Press. Printed and bound by McNaughton & Gunn, Inc., in the United
States of America.

ISBN: 978-1-939663-70-2

Available through D.A.P./Distributed Art Publishers
75 Broad Street, Suite 630
New York, New York 10004
Tel: (212) 627-1999
Fax: (212) 627-9484

10   9   8   7   6   5   4   3   2

CONTENTS

TRANSLATOR'S INTRODUCTION

Malpertuis is an extraordinary book by an extraordinary man.

The man: many authors have a myth or legend attached to them, which they more or less assiduously cultivate. Some have more of a myth than others, and Jean Ray was one such.

Almost at random one might cite: references to a Dakota Indian grandmother; a youth and early manhood serving on tramp steamers in the South Seas, the China Sea, the Gulf of Carpentaria, in the contraband trade, dealing in whatever came to hand, be it illegal mother-of-pearl or other, more unusual goods; hints of the odd bit of piracy; the reputation for being able to tame tarantulas, and for being no stranger to the lion tamer's cage; involvement in Rum Row, the offshore trade in liquor during the US Prohibition era, and bearing the scars of gunshot wounds received then . . .

Ray's friend, Thomas Owen (i.e., Gérald Bertot), another master of the uncanny story, and a guardian of the legend, wrote of him: "Jean Ray was a Gothic personality. He had about him a touch of the damned priest or the cathedral gargoyle. There was a 'stony' element in him, something that called to mind a prison wall, the vault of a tomb, in which one imagined sins, regrets, and sufferings buried. The icy indifference of quarried stones and mortar keeps all things secret. In that way the closed features of Jean Ray seemed to know nothing of what might be going on in his inmost self. A hard mask one never again forgot, once one had the good—or for some the bad—luck to see it face to face. Gothic, to be sure. Almost barbaric. Certainly cruel. One imagined the man as readily on a pyre, or at the foot of a pyre, torch in hand, a heretic or an executioner. He seemed suitable for both roles. His eyes were gray and cold, his lips thin and severe. The brow and profile of a Red Indian, but with a gray and wan complexion. Stony complexion, heart of stone. That man who, it seemed, scarcely belonged to the world of men could have been an executioner in Venice, a North Sea pirate, a Baltic trader, or a Chicago hit man . . .

"He had dabbled in everything. In medicine, in occultism, in magic. He spoke and wrote French, English, German, Flemish, and could get by in several other languages as well."

To what extent Ray manufactured his legend will doubtless remain something of a mystery, but he clearly must have had a hand in it. I strongly suspect his friends embroidered the story. That he rather enjoyed it is beyond doubt. Faced with questions, he liked to say: "Avec Jean Ray, on ne sait jamais" ("You never know with Jean Ray"). An Italian saying sums things up nicely: "Se non è vero, è ben trovato"—"It may not be true, but it's a good story."

So, what about the facts?

Raymond Jean-Marie de Kremer (Jean Ray) was born in Ghent/Gand, 8 July 1887; he died in that city 17 September 1964. His father was a minor official in the port, and his mother ran a girls' school. His school career was moderately distinguished but, for some reason or other, he failed to continue his university level studies. From 1910 to 1919 he worked in the city administration, mostly in lowly clerical posts. By now he was already writing—poems and lyrics for the local French and Flemish theaters.

By the early 1920s he was on the editorial team of the *Journal de Gand* and, later, of the monthly *L'Ami du Livre*.

1925 saw the publication of his first book, *Les Contes du Whisky* (*Whiskey Tales*), fantastical and uncanny stories in the vein that would characterize his best work.

In 1926, the setback: he was charged, along with the stockbroker for whom he was working, with embezzlement. One rumor had it—and here the legend seems to mingle with the somewhat problematical "facts"—that the money involved might have gone into an American bootlegging enterprise; another that it was to be siphoned off into the failed *Journal de Gand*. What seems certain is that Ray was to a large extent a fall guy and a victim of his own credulity, to say nothing of his taste for "le bluff." In January 1927, he was sentenced to six years imprisonment, but was released in 1929. While in jail he wrote two of his best long short stories, "The Gloomy Alley" and "The Mainz Psalter."

From now on *work*: and, with a "record," he had little chance of regular and respectable employment. Hence a constant stream of writing of every sort: straightforward journalism; stories in Flemish (by "John Flanders," the John being Jean, and the Flanders a tribute to Daniel Defoe's heroine Moll), many of these being in the same fantastic vein as those written as Jean Ray; stories for young readers, under a host of other pseudonyms, some of them downright grotesque—King Ray, Alix R. Bantam, Sailor, etc.; scenarios for comic strips; and, most importantly, between 1933 and 1940, the 100-odd *Adventures of Harry Dickson*, the American Sherlock Holmes. At the suggestion of an Amsterdam publisher, Ray undertook to translate from the German a mass of pre-1914 booklets recounting the exploits of a sub-Holmsean sleuth. Finding them poor beyond belief, he suggested he rewrite the series. This was accepted, on condition that each story take as its point of departure the original cover illustration, and that the length be much the same. Knocking them out anonymously on an ancient Underwood, often in a day and a night for some seventy typed pages and employing a technique that bordered upon automatic writing, Ray produced an oeuvre hovering between Nick Carter or Sexton Blake and H. P. Lovecraft (with Conan Doyle lurking in the background), whose content often presages his best work. Subsequently collected and published under Ray's own name, they have remained intermittently in print and number among their admirers the film director Alain Resnais.

The war put an end to Flanders/Ray/de Kremer's "alimentary" writing, but it left him free to publish the best of his work, in French, and under the name of Jean Ray: *Le Grand Nocturne* (*The Great Nocturnal*) (1942); *La Cité de l'Indicible Peur* (*The City of Unspeakable Fear*) (1943); *Malpertuis* (1943); *Les Cercles de L'Epouvante* (*Circles of Dread*) (1943); *Les Derniers Contes de Canterbury* (*The Last Canterbury Tales*) (1944); and, in 1947, *Le Livre des Fantômes* (*The Book of Ghosts*).

Sadly, after the Liberation, he found himself again on the literary treadmill. Much of his work in the immediate postwar years was in Flemish, and written for the younger reader of such series as "Vlaamse Filmkens." By 1948 he was already contributing to Tintin, "Le journal des jeunes de 7 à 77 ans." Simultaneously, as John Flanders, he was writing scenarios for a comic strip in *Het Volk*.

A letter, written in November 1950 by Ray to the cinéaste and writer Roland Stragliati, "accompanied by a curriculum vitae of a highly inventive nature," contributed largely to the diffusion of the Ray legend.

In April 1955 his wife of forty-three years died. By now, age was beginning to tell; he was occupying a ground floor flat in his daughter's house.

In December of that year, due in large measure to the intervention of Raymond Queneau and Stragliati, "who have moved heaven and earth to rescue *Malpertuis*, and indeed Jean Ray, from the obscurity of oblivion," *Malpertuis* was republished in France by the leading firm Denoël, in their mass-market S.F. paperback series "Présence du Futur."

It was in the winter of 1959/1960 that a memorable encounter took place at the house of Ray's friend Henri Vernes between Ray and Alain Resnais. Resnais had long wanted to make a film based on the character of Harry Dickson. The creator of *Hiroshima Mon Amour*, *L'Année Dernière à Marienbad*, and *Je t'aime, je t'aime* had run across some of the scruffy brochures in his boyhood in the 1930s in provincial Vannes, and the memory had stayed with him. As a filmmaker he had roamed the streets of London, the scene of many of the Dickson episodes, taking photographs—evocative location shots . . . Nothing came of the long-cherished project, but in 1974 Resnais published a book of these "repérages" with a commentary by Jorge Semprún.

Another meeting in 1960 was with Michel de Ghelderode (1898–1962), the Belgian dramatist whose world recalls that of Bosch and Brueghel, and who also wrote some stories that are masterpieces of the macabre. Not surprisingly, the two men became firm friends.

The autumn of 1963 saw the publication in Paris of the first volume of an *Oeuvres Complètes* (in four volumes) by Laffont—by no means complete, but the beginning of a torrent of publications from a succession of publishers which, over the succeeding years, would assure Ray's reputation.

He died, at home, on the morning of 17 September 1964.

A few weeks before his death, in a letter to a friend, Albert Van Hageland, he wrote his own mock epitaph:

> *Ci gît Jean Ray*
> *homme sinistre*
> *qui ne fut rien*
> *pas même ministre*

("Here lies Jean Ray / a gent sinister / who was nothing / not even a minister").

In their short and shrewd book on the detective story, the Boileau-Narcejac team come up with a neat formulation: "La peur est la face d'ombre du cogito"—"Fear is the dark side of [Descartes's] cogito." Or, crudely paraphrased: I fear, therefore I am. Fear—of death, of all sorts of supernatural manifestations, of crime—is universal. If the ghosts don't get me, the crooks will. Hence the ever-present undercurrent of fear in human awareness. Science never fully does away with magical thinking: superstition lurks in the shadows of official religion, rationality never quite overcomes the irrational. Hence, consequently and paradoxically, the obscure attraction of that very same underlying fear. And so too the persistence of the tale of terror, from the oldest folklore down to the Gothic novel, the horror comic, and the literature of crime; more specifically, the kind of literature exemplified by such writers as H. P. Lovecraft and Jean Ray.

Malpertuis is Jean Ray's only really full-length novel. It is also, on his own assertion, the fruit of years of careful work, planning, and revision: "ten years, perhaps twelve, of nights and voyages, over the whole world. I wrote, discarded, burnt, then the scissors and the glue pot came into play with the survivors." *Malpertuis* is also his masterpiece, to say nothing of being one of the masterpieces of fantastic literature as such, in any language.

Fantastic literature, or at all events, that in which the fear-element is prominent, overlaps as a class with the mystery story (of which, of course, the detective story is a subclass—who doesn't fear being arbitrarily snuffed?). In the case of the mystery story in the wider sense, as distinct from the classical whodunit, it does not necessarily matter much if the reader knows, at least in outline, the "solution" of the mystery. The fascination lies in seeing the story unfold, spotting the clues, or trying to catch the small verbal hints in the text. So it is of no great importance if the reader of *Malpertuis* is aware from the start—albeit in a fairly vague way—that the story involves . . . but perhaps it is not quite fair to reveal any more here.

It is only by degrees that the mystery is clarified and the reader comes to see with what amazing patience and craftsmanship Ray constructed the narrative mechanism into which he or she is relentlessly drawn. Throughout the text, with its proliferation of successive narrators and its Chinese box structure, not to mention the variety of themes, everything is portioned out; everything has its place and its significance. The clues are there, strategically placed, and when the *dénouement* is reached, the reader realizes that he or she has subconsciously noticed them, without necessarily grasping their significance. The result is a peculiar and subtle kind of satisfaction.

Iain White

MALPERTUIS

I dedicate this book to my good friend and colleague
Jules Stéphane, one of the Auteurs Associés.[1]
For Stanislas-André Steeman, another of the Auteurs Associés:
On page 113 of your *Le Mannequin assassiné* you wrote:
"This house should be cast to the ground:
It looks like a monstrous candlesnuffer to me.
The past is eating it away like cancer.
Yet I can't blow up the barracks,
like we tried to do when we were kids."
These words, Steeman, haunt me.[2]
I should set *Malpertuis* under their sign
if I had the right. But were the most formidable missiles
to detonate in its shadow,
they wouldn't even make the windowpanes of its facade shake.

J. R.

AN INVENTORY, BY WAY OF PREFACE AND EXPLANATION

The job on the monastery of the White Fathers was definitely worth the trouble.

I could, had I so wished, have made a clean sweep of any amount of valuables, but although lacking in devoutness, I am not an unbeliever and the very idea of making away with devotional objects, even though they be weighty objects of gold and silver, fills me with horror.

The good monks will be weeping over the loss of their palimpsests, their incunabula, and their antiphonaries, but they praise the Lord for His having turned away an impious hand from their ciboria and their monstrances.

My impression was that the weighty pewter tube I found concealed in the monastery must contain some valuable manuscripts for which an unscrupulous collector might give me a tidy sum; but all I found therein was a crabbed scrawl, the laborious decipherment of which I put off until a later date.

The leisure this called for came to me when the proceeds of my expedition transformed me into a comfortable citizen of tranquil and orderly aspirations; it takes money to turn a ruffian into an honest man, obedient to the law.

As regards myself, I feel obliged to provide certain explanations. They will be brief—for my part in this story calls for some discretion.

My family had intended me for the teaching profession. I had obtained a place at the École normale, where I was an apt pupil. I greatly regret not being able to make anything of the philological thesis that won me the congratulations of the examiners. But it explains the interest I took in my discovery and the obstinacy I brought to the solution of a problem, for which the data were appallingly obscure. If I was recompensed in a most fantastic fashion, that surely is no fault of mine.

When I had emptied the pewter tube and saw my table strewn with yellowing, scribbled papers, it needed a return to the patience and Benedictine curiosity of my youth to set me to my task. At first this was no more than an inventory.

As a matter of fact, all those sheets of paper would, if they had been gathered together and submitted to a publisher, have constituted a work of colossal size and minimal interest, so encumbered were they with useless digressions, extraordinary observations, and such a display of dubious speculations.

It was up to me to sift, to classify, to eliminate.

Four hands, trembling, fevered—if not five—have participated in the putting together of this narrative of mystery and terror.

The first was that of an adventurer of genius who was also a man of the Church—for he wore a priest's garb. I shall call him Doucedame the Elder to distinguish him from one of his descendants of the same name, who likewise wore the Cloth: the Abbé Doucedame. The latter was a saintly priest and worthy of veneration. He too collaborated in the annals relating the history of Malpertuis. He was, in a sense, the torchbearer of truth in that haunted darkness. Thus Doucedame the Elder is the first of the four—or five—authors of the account, and the younger Doucedame is the third. According to my calculations the adventure of Doucedame the Elder took place in the first quarter of the previous century; the light thrown on the affair by his grandson seems to have been lit in the beginning of the last quarter.

A young man of excellent education and, in my opinion, of highly cultivated tastes, but marked with the brand of misfortune is the second author of the narrative. It is to him that we are indebted for the kernel of the story.

It is about him that the whole story gravitates in tumultuous and fearsome orbits. Reading the first pages in his hand I thought this was a journal like those kept, in the last century, by young persons fired by a reading of Sterne's *Sentimental Journey*. I was undeceived as, slowly, my work progressed. I discovered then that he had committed his thoughts to paper only when in distress, when faced with an imminent farewell to life.

A little notebook, in a neat, scholarly hand, was also in the metal sheath, bringing the number of collaborators to four.

This was in the hand of Dom Misseron, the deceased Abbot of the monastery of the White Fathers in which I had carried out the profitable excursion that led me to the discovery of the pewter tube. At the end of the notebook a date was written: it was, as it were, a fixed point, rigidly immobile in the headlong flight of time: 26 September 1898!

Fifthly—and finally—I'm obliged to add my own name to the roll of those Scribes who, without their knowledge (or almost without it), have given Malpertuis a place in the history of human terror.

~~~✕

At the head of this narrative I place a brief chapter whose author, even though he does not speak in the first person, is undoubtedly

Doucedame the Elder. The identity of the handwriting with that of other lines known to have been written by that man of profound learning (but somberly malign disposition) convinces me of this. As I see it, the renegade priest had decided to write a true adventure story, presented in an objective fashion, in which his own person would not be spared any more than those of the rest—in which indeed, on the contrary, it would be his cynical pleasure to besmear himself with shady villainies.

But the disorder of his life led him, no doubt, to give up his ambition to be a scribbler and he was content to leave a few lines— which are nonetheless of great interest in the history of Malpertuis.

I have retained the title he gave to that beginning of a story, which I reproduce here, just as it stands:

PART I: ALECTA

OPENING

The Vision of Anacharsis

> *It is in vain that you build churches, stake out the roads with chapels and crosses; you will not prevent the gods of ancient Thessaly from returning in the songs of poets and the books of scholars.*
>
> —Hawthorne[3]

The fog broke and the island, whose presence the fury of the breakers had already announced from afar, seemed so terrifying that the mariner Anacharsis, clinging to the wheel, began to cry out in alarm.

For many hours his tartane, the Fena,[4] *had been heading for disaster, drawn by the deadly lodestone of that monstrous rock, battered by the high and livid waves and crowned by the lightning's flamboyant rage.*

Anacharsis cried out, for he was afraid of the death he had seen about him since dawn. The fall of the lateen-yard had killed his pilot, Mirales; and when the little boat took a list to starboard, and the water they had taken aboard flowed back, he had seen the corpse of the cabin boy Estopoulos, his head caught in a scupper.

The Fena *had not been responding to her rudder since the evening before, and the skipper's navigation was purely instinctive.*

He realized that he had completely lost his bearings, as much by drifting as by the contrary winds and unknown tides. He had no recollection of ever having seen this island, although the seas there-abouts had for many years been familiar to him.

The horrible stench of anagyris,[5] the thrice-accursed plant, came to him from that mortal land, already so close at hand, and he knew that impure spirits were involved in his adventure.

Of this he was quite certain when he saw forms floating over the summits of the rock. In their shapes and attitudes they were repulsively human, and for the most part they were gigantic beyond comparison.

They gave the impression of being of different sexes, to judge by the strength of some and the relative beauty of others. Their dimensions too differed among themselves; some approached the normal in size, others seemed dwarfed and deformed, but it may be that distance played a part in these discrepancies of vision.

Immobile every one, they were staring fixedly into the tormented sky, frozen in a horrible despair.

"Corpses!" he sobbed. "Corpses the size of mountains!"

And in terror he turned his gaze away from one of them which, in its formidable immobility, remained tinged with an indescribable majesty.

Another did not float but was as one with the rock. It was distorted with agony and inhuman suffering; its flank gaped open like a cavern, and it alone seemed to have preserved some dreadful shudderings of life and motion. A shadow was hovering over it, but since it was obscured from time to time by wisps of fog, the mariner was unable to assign to it a distinct identity. For all that he would have sworn it was an enormous bird. It rose and fell at the rough wind's pleasure. Nevertheless it was plain that it was watching with a ferocious avidity over the captive form of the rock. At one moment it even fell from on

JEAN RAY

high onto its phantasmal prey and cruelly tore at it with claws and beak.

A whirlwind caught the tartane, set it twisting like a spinning top and hurled it beyond the breakers. The jiggermast and the bowsprit were ripped away and the cabin boy's body swept overboard.

A spar fell on Anacharsis, striking him on the back of the neck.

For a time he lost all awareness and, when he regained his senses, he was no longer at the wheel but clinging to a stump of the mast.

He could no longer see the island, nor the hideous floating forms; but a ferocious figure hung over him.

Face to face with those cruel eyes and curled-up lips he cried out again. But an instant later he was aware that he had nothing to fear from them, for they belonged to a figurehead, horribly ugly to be sure, but lacking any murderous intention.

The figure surmounted a high, sharp prow, looming athwartships over the larboard side; a second later the Fena was rammed with a shattering blow and went under.

But somebody on the colliding ship had seen the mariner and a carefully manipulated grapnel delivered him from the perils of the sea.

Anacharsis was in pain, in terrible pain. His ribs were broken and his sides hurt him dreadfully. His hair and his beard were sopping with blood; but he smiled to find himself stretched out on a sailor's bunk in a narrow cabin lit by a lamp fixed to the compass mounting. There were men standing about, looking at him and talking among themselves.

One of them, an enormous mulatto, was scratching his vigorous black shock of hair with an expression of puzzlement.

"Devil take me," he bellowed, "if I thought I'd run into a little tub like that in these waters. What d'you make of it?"

The person to whom he addressed his query seemed no less surprised.

"Better ask the fellow," he growled. "But then like as not he'll talk some gibberish we don't understand. Better call in that blackguard Doucedame: he's a scholar, and if he isn't soused out of his mind he'll make something out of it."

Anacharsis saw a grossly fat creature bearing down on him, a man with a furfuraceous visage and malicious, squinting eyes who, by way of greeting, stuck out his tongue.

He spoke to him in his own language—that of the islanders of the archipelago.

"What are you up to in these parts?"

Anacharsis was hard pressed to collect his thoughts, much less to speak. It was as if a mountain were bearing down on his chest; to oblige his rescuers, though, he mastered his pain.

After a fashion he told his tale—his losing his way, the terrible storm that had wrecked the Fena, far from familiar waters.

"Tell me your name," the man they called Doucedame demanded.

"Anacharsis!"

"Eh? What's that you said? Tell me again!" the fat man exclaimed.

"Anacharsis! That's what my father was called, and it's my name too . . ."

"God almighty!" the fat man said, turning to his companions.

"What's all this got to do with us, Doucedame?" one of them asked.

"If that isn't a case of predestination, I'm a monkey's uncle!"

"Explain yourself, gutbag!" the mulatto commanded.

"Patience, Monsieur Anselme," the portly one replied with a respect touched with irony. "I must have recourse to my memory and my knowledge."

"The hell with the two of them, you gallows bird of a schoolmaster," Monsieur Anselme intoned.

"Anacharsis," Doucedame explained, bowing to an invisible interlocutor, "is the name of the Scythian philosopher who, having sailed among the islands of Attica, came to Athens in the sixth century before Christ, where he sought to introduce the worship of Demeter along with that of Pluto. It cost him dear, for it is never prudent to involve oneself in religious matters. They strangled him."

The skipper of the Fena, who understood nothing of this blather and who felt his strength slipping away, interrupted him to speak of the terrible forms he had glimpsed among the mists swirling about the island.

Forthwith Doucedame began shouting and gesticulating.

"We're there!" he chuckled. "I guarantee you a cargo of gold, my friends! Anacharsis, the representative of the gods, is doomed, down to the last of his descendants, to achieve his mission. Ah! centuries and millennia are as nothing to phantoms . . ."

Monsieur Anselme had grown serious.

"Have him tell us the course he was on at the end," he said.

"Due south," the wounded man said when Doucedame had translated.

"And what are we to do now?"

"We can't burden ourselves with useless passengers," Monsieur Anselme announced firmly.

The fat Doucedame exploded with laughter: "It is written that the line of Anacharsis meet their end by strangulation!"

Anacharis understood nothing of this talk, but he read his fate in the inexorable expressions of those to whom he was indebted for an hour of existence.

He murmured a prayer—one he did not complete in this life.

Before submitting to the reader the continuation of Doucedame the Elder's account, I shall insert here the narrative of Jean-Jacques Grandsire. As I have already pointed out, this narrative constitutes the kernel of the story. It is, in short, around the appalling destiny of Jean-Jacques Grandsire that the whole horror of Malpertuis revolves.

1

Uncle Cassave Passes On

> *The man who enters upon the mystery of death, leaving to the living the mystery of his life, has at the same time cheated both life and death.*
>
> —Stefano Zannowich[6]

Uncle Cassave is dying.

White and quivering, his beard flows from his leaden face over the red eiderdown. He breathes the air as if he were inhaling utterly delectable odors and his hands, which are large and hairy, claw at anything that comes within their reach.

The Griboin woman, who came to bring him his tea with lemon, said: "He's packing his little bags."

Uncle Cassave had heard her.

"Not yet, woman, not yet." He laughed humorlessly.

When she had gone, in an eddy of frightened petticoats, he turned and spoke to me.

"I haven't got all that long left now, my boy; but then again, dying's a serious business, so one shouldn't be in a rush about it."

Then once more his gaze began to wander about the room, lingering on each object as if for a final inventory.

One after another it rests on an imitation bronze theorbo-player, a minuscule, hazy Adriaen Brouwer, a cheap engraving representing an old woman, and a very valuable *Amphitrite* by Mabuse.[7]

There is a knock at the door and Uncle Dideloo enters.

"Good day, Great Uncle," he says.

He is the one member of our family to call Uncle Cassave "Great Uncle."

Dideloo is a civil servant and a meticulous man. He had started out as a teacher, but his pupils used to persecute him.

Now he is a deputy chief clerk in the local administration, and for the copy clerks working under his orders a worse tyrant is not to be found.

"Charles," Uncle Cassave says, "talk to me—make a speech."

"Certainly, Great Uncle, but I'm worried that might tire you."

"In that case admire me in silence. But look sharp about it. I don't much like the look of you."

Old Cassave is turning nasty.

"I'm sorry to have to say it," Uncle Dideloo sighs, "but I have to talk to you about wretched materialistic questions, Great Uncle. We need money..."

"Really! That's surprising!"

"We have to pay the doctor..."

"Sambucus? Oh, come now! You give him his food and his drink, and you let him sleep on the sofa in the drawing room if need be. He won't ask for more than that."

"The apothecary..."

"I never finish any of his bottles, and I never touch his powders. The fact is that your wife, charming Sylvie, who suffers from every ailment in the medical dictionary, makes off with the lot."

"There are many other things as well, Great Uncle ... Where are we to find the money?"

"In the third cellar, under the seventh flagstone, nine feet four inches down, there is a strongbox filled with gold. Will that do?"

"What a man!" Uncle Dideloo whimpers.

"I'm truly sorry I can't say the same thing of yourself, Dideloo. And now be off with you . . . eh! fathead!"

Charles Dideloo casts me a menacing look and sneaks out of the room, so small and thin that he barely has to open the door.

I am seated in a tasseled and thickly upholstered armchair, my face turned toward the bed.

Uncle Cassave returns my gaze.

"Turn a little more into the light, Jean-Jacques."

I obey. The dying man stares at me with painfully close attention.

"There's no denying it," he murmurs after a prolonged examination, "You're a Grandsire, despite the loss of character in your features. It only needed a touch of softness in the blood to mellow the harshness of your ancestors.

"Dammit though, your grandfather Anselme Grandsire—Monsieur Anselme as they called him in days gone by—was no end of a rogue!"

Coming from Uncle Cassave, the insult was a familiar one, and I thought no worse of him on that account, for I had never known my ill-famed grandfather.

"If he hadn't died of beriberi on the Guinea Coast, he'd have become an even greater rogue," Uncle Cassave continues, laughing. "He was a man who loved perfection in all things!"

The door opens wide and my sister Nancy appears.

Her dress is skin tight, emphasizing her splendid curves: her deeply scalloped corsage leaves no doubt as to the richness of her flesh.

Her face, dark and flushed, gives evidence to her anger.

"You've sent Uncle Charles packing," she says. "That's all well and good, let him look after his own affairs. But he was right: we need money."

"You and he," Uncle Cassave replies, "are two entirely different things."

"Good. So where is it then?" Nancy frets. "The Griboins haven't any more and the tradesmen are sending in their bills."

"All you have to do is to take it from the shop!"

Nancy laughs—a strident little laugh that goes well with her haughty style of beauty.

"Since seven this morning we've had six customers—a total of forty-two *sous.*"

"And they say business is looking up!" the old man chuckles. "But don't trouble yourself about that, my lovely. Go back to the shop. Take the little stepladder with seven steps and climb up to the seventh. Don't do it when there's a customer in the shop, though— you wear your skirts very short. Being the height you are, perched on the seventh step you'll be able to reach the tin box marked 'Raw Sienna.' Shove your pretty white hands into that uninviting powder, my sweet, and you'll find four or five rolls that are heavy for their size. Wait a moment now. Don't be in such a hurry. I like having you here. If the Sienna gets under your fingernails it'll take you hours before you're rid of it. Right you are, then! Off you go, my beauty! And if Mathias Krook pinches your backside on the stairs, where it's dark, there's no use shouting out. I won't be coming."

Nancy sticks out her tongue, red and pointed as a flame, and leaves, banging the door behind her.

For a few moments we hear her heels rat-tat-tatting on the sonorous treads of the staircase; then her voice, loud and furious.

"Pig!"

Uncle Cassave laughs.

"That's not Mathias!" he says.

A slap echoes.

"It's Uncle Charles!"

The old man is in fine fettle and, were it not for his leaden color and the labored, bellows-sound of his breathing, I would never think him to be dying.

"She at least is worthy of her rogue of a grandfather," he declares with evident satisfaction.

Silence falls again in the room. The bellows are animating an invisible brazier. The hands claw at the sheets with a sound like that of a file.

"Jean-Jacques?"

"Uncle Cassave?"

"Did you get news this morning, Nancy and yourself, of your father, Nicolas Grandsire?"

"Yesterday morning, Uncle."

"Good, Good . . . the days don't mean very much to me. Where did it come from, that letter?"

"Singapore. Daddy is doing well."

"Always supposing he hasn't been hanged in the twelve weeks the letter took in coming. God help us, if he were ever to come back! . . ."

He reflects, his head bent over one shoulder, like a strange carrion crow.

"He'll never be back ... Why should he after all? The Grandsires were born to sail the high seas under all the world's winds, not to go moldy under a roof."

The door opens. Nancy has returned, smiling, her ill humor gone.

"I found five rolls, Uncle Cassave," she says.

"Heavy stuff, gold, eh?" Uncle Cassave sniggers. "I suppose you know what to do with it?"

"Don't I just know!" Nancy replies pertly.

She leaves us, and as she shuts the door she calls out to me: "Jiji—Elodie's waiting for you in the kitchen."

We hear her on the stairs, laughing softly and clucking like a hen.

"This time it's Mathias," Uncle says.

He laughs heartily, even though this unleashes a tempest of rattling in the depths of his chest.

"Five rolls she said, eh? There were six of them! Aha! She's a splendid little granddaughter for that ruffian of an Anselme Grandsire . . . I'm really pleased!"

These visits, his pleasure, and his talking have visibly tired him.

"Go and see Elodie, my boy," he says in a voice that has suddenly grown weary and remote.

I'm more than happy to do so; from the depths of the huge and Stygian cellarage, where there is a vast kitchen the size of a lecture hall, rises the warm smell of waffles and the fine scent of melted butter augmented with sugar and cinnamon.

I traverse an enormously long corridor at the end of which is a square of feeble light.

At the far end of a vestibule bathed in the shifting glow of gaslight one could see a shop, distant and unreal, as if seen from the wrong end of a spyglass.

The story of that shop, tacked onto a rich and powerful master mariner's house, is a strange one; but I shall soon enough have occasion to return to it . . .

I see a high wooden counter, tall carboys, bunches of paper bags, and the silhouettes of Nancy and the assistant Mathias, close to each other, perhaps too close . . .

But for me the spectacle is of little interest. The urgent call of the kitchen is much more imperious than that of idle adolescent curiosity.

The song of the cooking butter and the clatter of the waffle irons imposes their joyful note on the evening's calm twilight.

"It was high time you came," our old servant Elodie cries. "The doctor was just going to eat your share."

"They're very good," a small voice chortles from the shadows, "well sugared, the way I like them."

There is no gaslight in the kitchen. Uncle Cassave had reserved that one luxury for the shop; a broad-wicked lamp casts a penurious light on the table and the whiteness of the plates. A candle on the mantle shelf, guttering in the hot blast of the stove, illuminates the heavy, black waffle iron.

"How's the patient doing?" the small voice continues. "Very nicely, eh?"

"Is he going to get well, doctor?"

"Get well? Whoever told you such a thing! No, no . . . Cassave is well and truly condemned by the Faculty. That doesn't prevent me, though, from doing something for him."

In the lamplight a decrepit hand, wax pale, brandishes a sheet of paper.

"Here's the death certificate and the authorization for burial *ad hoc*, drawn up and duly signed by myself. I've left only the date blank. Yesterday it still had double pneumonia as the cause of death. But I've given the matter some thought and it seems to me Bright's disease would be more distinguished.

"I owe that much to old Cassave, don't you think? And now, Elodie, I'd very much like another of those excellent waffles."

Thus speaks Doctor Sambucus, whose visits Uncle accepts and whose prescriptions he refuses.

He is so small, so puny, that even with his hat on his head he barely reaches up to Elodie's nose, and she was no great height.

His face is a mass of wrinkles and scars—except for his nose, which juts out from that rumpled miniature like a pink, fleshy headland.

The waxen hand takes on an extraordinary firmness as it cuts the waffle into regular squares before saturating them with butter and syrup.

"I believe I'm the older of the two of us, although one can't say anything at all precise about the dear man; but I think he'll be the first to go," the greedy old man cackles cheerfully. "That's a consolation to a man of my age, for it seems to me that death is forgetting us. Who knows? Perhaps that's how it is … It's forty years now since Cassave and I became close friends. I made his acquaintance on a ferryboat. He'd been hunting and he'd shot a brace of godwit. I congratulated him because they're splendid birds and difficult to shoot.

"He invited me to share them with him. I took good care not to refuse his offer: a fine, fat godwit is even tastier than its relative, the woodcock.

"Since then I have had free access to Malpertuis."

Malpertuis! For the first time the name has flowed in a turbid ink from my terrified pen! That house, placed by the most terrible of wills like a full stop at the end of so many human destinies—I still thrust aside its image! I recoil, I procrastinate rather than bring it to the forefront of my memory!

What is more, pressed no doubt by the brevity of their earthly term, human beings are less patient than the house; *things* remain after them, *things*—like the stones of which accursed dwellings are made. Human beings are animated by the feverish haste of sleep tumbling through abattoir gates—they will not rest until they have taken their place under the great candlesnuffer that is Malpertuis.

Nancy swans into the kitchen; she preferred *crêpes* to waffles, and would tear them between her cruel teeth like scraps of burning skin.

"Doctor Sambucus," she inquires, "when will Uncle Cassave die? You must know."

"Flower of my dreams," the old doctor replies, "are you addressing Aesculapius or Tiresias? The healer or the soothsayer?"

"It doesn't matter which, provided he knows."

Sambucus picks and plucks at the air with his waxen fingers: he calls this operation taking his bearings by the celestial planisphere.

"The pole star is in place as always. That's the only one attuned with the infinite. Aldebaran is rising to larboard, under the Pleiades. Saturn is prowling the horizon he poisons with his luminous cyanide.

"Half a turn . . . The South is more communicative than the North today. Pegasus has a whiff of the stable of old Helicon. Cygnus is singing as if her ascent to the zenith is going to be the death of her; the Eagle, the fires of Altair in his eyes, is winging the airs closest to the God of Space; Aquarius is up to no good, and Capricorn . . ."

"That's enough," my sister breaks in impatiently; "as always, you know nothing."

"In my days," the doctor continues, abruptly changing the subject, "they used to scent waffles with *eau de naffe*;[8] the gods themselves never knew a more delicious treat. Ah yes, my rose! You're asking about the excellent Cassave. He has another week to go at least, if not two, before he casts his soul loose among the stars."

"Ass!" my sister says. "Three days will be enough."

My sister was right.

The Griboin woman pokes her head into the kitchen.

"Mam'zelle Nancy, the Misses Cormélon are here . . ."

"Put them in the yellow drawing room . . ."

"But Mam'zelle, there's no fire!"

"Exactly, that's why!"

"There's Madame Sylvie too, and her daughter, come to fetch Monsieur Charles."

"The yellow drawing room!"

At that point I rebel.

"But Euryale is with Aunt Sylvie!"

"What about it? Euryale doesn't bother herself in the slightest, burning hot or freezing, storm or flat calm . . . I suppose Cousin Philarète is there at least?"

"He's with us in our kitchen, Mam'zelle Nancy; he's drinking Calvados with Griboin—he says he's got a cold on his stomach."

"Did he finish the job for Uncle Cassave? If he didn't, show him the door."

"The stuffed mouse? Oh yes, Mam'zelle! He's brought it along with him, and he's made a good job of it."

Doctor Sambucus breaks into a low, gurgling, and protracted laugh.

"That'll be the brave Cassave's last hunting piece! A mouse it was, that ran over the eiderdown. He throttled it neatly, between his thumb and his forefinger. Forty years ago he was still shooting godwits . . . heh, heh, heh!"

"Everyone into the yellow drawing room!" Nancy commands. "I've got something to say to those people."

Shabby and down at heel, the Griboin woman slips away.

"Me too?" the little doctor asks wearily.

"Yes, finish your waffle."

"In that case I'll grab a cup of coffee with some rum in it and plenty of sugar. At my age, a session in the yellow drawing room is like taking a siesta on a glacier," Sambucus grumbles.

Of all the sinister and icy rooms that go to make up the interior of Malpertuis, the yellow drawing room is the most sinister and icy.

The two seven-branched candelabra that light it do so poorly enough; but I am certain that Nancy will have lit no more than three or four wicks.

The company who assemble there seat themselves on high, straight-backed chairs; indistinct shadows whose voices fall flat, like a clamor lost in a desert, and every word they say is lugubrious, ill intentioned, or despairing.

Nancy makes off with the broad-wicked lamp, for at this hour the corridors are thick with darkness. She sets it down several meters from the door, on the pedestal of a statue of the boundary god; she has no intention of providing any extra illumination for all these people she detests.

"I'll leave you the candle, Elodie."

"That will be enough for me to say my rosary by."

The assembly in the yellow drawing room is exactly as I expected—made up of dark and indistinct shadows.

Installed in the one low chair in the form of a prayer stool, it takes me a bit of time to recognize them.

Veiled in perpetual mourning, the Cormélon sisters occupy a sofa upholstered in black repp; they look like three praying mantises lying in wait for some nocturnal insect to come within their range.

They don't greet anyone, stiff and motionless, but I feel their eyes fixed with cold fury on our entrance.

From the open door Cousin Philarète, uncouth looking and badly dressed, cries out: "Hello everybody! Would you like to see my mouse?"

He holds aloft a small board. To it is glued a gray and pink form.

"I'd have liked to have mounted it sitting up like a squirrel, but it wouldn't come right that way. Didn't even look pretty." He speaks with the coarse joviality of the uneducated.

The Dideloo family sit in the zone of light about the candlesticks.

Uncle Charles stares stubbornly at his brightly polished boots; Aunt Sylvie, commonplace, neuter, graying, grins at us, slack-lipped, and at her least movement the jet-bejeweled breastplate of her corsage judders and creaks.

I have eyes only for their daughter, my Cousin Euryale, dressed with a nun-like modesty but with her amazing mass of chestnut red hair that seems sprinkled with shifting stars, and her eyes of jade.

She keeps her eyes closed, and I regret that; I should have liked to have played with them—as one plays with gems, rolling them between one's fingers—awakening their latent green flames, breathing life into them.

Suddenly a shrewish voice arises.

"We want to see Uncle Cassave!"

It is Eléonore, the eldest of the Cormélon sisters.

"You'll all see him in three days, and for the last time. He will have something to say to you. The notary Schampe will be present, and Father Eisengott too, as a witness. That is what Uncle Cassave wants."

Nancy has spoken without pausing for breath; now she falls silent, staring at the candle flames.

"It'll be for the will, I suppose?" Eléonore Cormélon asks.

Nancy makes no reply.

"I'd dearly have loved to have seen him," says Cousin Philarète. "He'd surely have complimented me on my mouse. But what he wants is what he wants, and it's not up to me to question it."

"Now that we're all together . . ." Uncle Charles begins.

"We? Don't speak of us as a whole or something that's connected!" my sister retorts. "And supposing we *are* all together, it isn't to talk to you. Now that you know what you have to know, you might as well be on your way."

"Do you realize, Mademoiselle, that it's taken us more than half an hour to get here?" cries Rosalie, the second of the sisters.

"As far as I'm concerned," Nancy replies with an ill-conceived fury, "you could've come here from the other side of the globe—and you could go back there!"

A look of uneasy attention comes abruptly over the faces of all those present—except Euryale's. Heavy footsteps sound hollowly on the tiled floor of the hallway; then the door opens, creaking on its hinges.

"Where does he hide?" comes a plaintive voice, "the one who's always putting out the lamps?"

"My God! . . . the lamps are going out again!" Aunt Sylvie wails.

"There was a lamp by the boundary god, and just as I was going toward it—it was such a cheerful sight—*he* blew it out . . ."

"Who is it then?" implores Aunt Dideloo.

"Who knows? I've never set out to see him because I know he's black and terrible. He puts out all the lamps. The pink and green one that lights the stairs up in such pretty colors was burning on the landing. A hand pinched the wick and night flowed down the staircase like the waters of Hell. I've been looking for him these five years, ten years, maybe all my life, but I never find him. Did I say I want to? No, no . . . I don't think I want to at all. But he's always putting the lamps out; he blows them out or pinches the flame to death . . ."

A strange man has just entered. He is immensely tall, horrifyingly thin—if he had not been bent, he would be well over six feet in height. A reddish greatcoat floats about this skeletal creature; his features are obscured in a repulsive, coarse mop of hair.

He draws close to the candles, ravished with delight.

"Aha! He doesn't put these out . . . not these ones . . . It's good to see the light . . . for me it's food and drink."

"Lampernisse, tenebrio . . . what are you doing here?" Doctor Sambucus calls out.

"He has every right to be here," Nancy ripostes. "He'll be at the coming assembly."

"There'll be candles alight . . . and lamps!" the old monster exults. "A light burns in my shop, as beautiful as the day, but I cannot return there. Such is the decree of the forces . . ."

"Lampernisse . . ." Uncle Dideloo begins, barely repressing a shudder of fear or of disgust.

"Lampernisse? It's my name . . . Lampernisse, Colors and Varnishes, that's what it said above the door in beautiful letters in three shades. I sold every sort of color, every sort . . . fumigating candles, drying oil, shale oil, gray and white mastic, ochre, zinc white and lead white, thick and creamy, clear varnish and brown varnish, French chalk and corrosive acids. My name's Lampernisse and I enjoy colors. Now they've put me in the darkness. There was a time I sold animal black and lampblack, but I never gave anyone the darkness of night. I am Lampernisse. I'm good and they've cast me into the depths of the night, with someone who always puts out the lamps!"

Now the monster is laughing and weeping at the same time. He holds out his spider-like hands to the candle flames. They burn his fingernails, but he pays no heed and continues to give rein to his pathetic joy.

I have no fear of Lampernisse, who lives somewhere in the house, somewhere they're hardly likely to look for him: the Griboins limit themselves to, once a day, putting out a basin of some sort of gruel on the upper part of one of the staircases, which he empties from time to time.

But the others seem to be cowering into themselves, as if from some evil approach. Only Nancy and Euryale show no reaction.

My sister relieves Sambucus of his cup, which is chattering horribly on its saucer. My cousin is feigning sleep, but there is a glimmer of green fire under her closed eyelids: she must be watching the lamentable apparition of the tenebrio.

"Be on your ways," Nancy says bruskly, addressing the whole company.

"You're most polite, Mademoiselle," Elénore Cormélon grates out.

"Are you waiting for me to have you thrown out?"

"Nancy!" Uncle Dideloo interpolates, "I beg you . . ."

"You . . . you . . . ," Nancy growls, "you'll hold your tongue and be the first to go."

"So you're in charge here, Mademoiselle Grandsire?" Rosalie Cormélon asks.

"It's taken you some time to grasp it."

"She lights the candles," Lampernisse exclaims, "and they're candles that don't go out. Nobody blows them out. May she be blessed!"

He is dancing about in the light, projecting on the far wall an ungainly shadow which Philarète—who is supposedly not quite all there—in the fever of these brief and disagreeable events tries to avoid, as if it were tangible and malevolent.

"My colors!" Lampernisse cries, dancing with renewed vigor before the minuscule bonfires. "They're all there! I shan't sell them, and nobody else can . . ."

He takes on a perplexed look and, from the depths of his filthy, gray mane, his eyes beseech Nancy.

". . . unless it's the one who puts out the lamps . . . Oh, Goddess!"

With a gesture Nancy cut short the assembly—the gesture of a reaper laying low the standing corn.

"We shall see each other in three days."

The shadows advanced toward the door with the slow pace of processionaries. Euryale followed in her mother's footsteps; she had opened her eyes, but their green flame was lifeless now and she seemed scarcely to see.

Uncle Dideloo hesitated a moment on the threshold. I had the impression he wanted to say something to Nancy and then thought better of it and slipped into the darkness of the hallway. The short halt cost him his place in the line and Alice, the youngest of the Misses Cormélon, overtook him.

Suddenly I heard a cry of pain.

Nancy broke into a tiny peal of strident laughter.

"His mania has him in its grasp now!" she giggled.

Doctor Sambucus had unearthed a thin bamboo cane from somewhere or other and was mercilessly laying into the wretched Lampernisse.

"Oh! ah!" the gray puppet lamented, "the devils are always beating me. They want my colors. But I haven't got them anymore . . . and they beat me . . . they beat me . . ."

Crying out as he went, he rushed up the staircase.

We saw his misshapen silhouette glide, simian, over the walls lit up by the lamps ranged from landing to landing.

"There's another!" he yelled suddenly.

Something black and formless flickered over the walls and the high, leaded windows.

"And another, and another . . . Oh! . . . it's there and I can't see it! Light and colors! He's taken them and left me in darkness . . ."

"Everybody come into the kitchen," Nancy commanded. "The madman is telling the truth. The thing that puts out the lamps is there!"

Somebody in the darkness, I don't know who, repeated slowly: "The-thing-that-puts-out-the-lamps . . ."

Nancy shrugged her shoulders. I have always loved my sister dearly, but she has always baffled me. Through all the events that have shaken us like twigs in a squall, it seems to me that women have been more level headed than men. Alas! from my very first steps into this world of mysteries I have stumbled into conjectures, and even perhaps into accusing my sister of indifference; for, if she had known, would she not perhaps have been able to thwart the most fatal of destinies?

"Very well then," said Elodie, laying aside her rosary. And then, without saying a word, she set the wine to heat with sugar and spices.

"It's a fine evening," Sambucus said. "What would you say, you young people, to a midnight meal? Old Cassave used to love one. Food and drink take on an extra flavor and aroma at midnight. We owe that discovery to the wisdom of the ancients."

The midnight meal was a respectable repast and, a tongue in sauce being served, Doctor Sambucus took advantage of the situation to inform us of the banquet given by Xanthus the Phrygian at which Aesop was served tongues of every kind, and only tongues, proclaiming them at once the greatest and worst delicacy.

Having seen Sambucus satiated and bloated as a little python, Nancy retired to her room; Elodie and I kept watch over the sleeping Cassave.

For the night he had donned a skullcap of Bergamo fabric embroidered with golden floss that gave him, by the glow of the floating wick of the nightlight, so grotesque an air that I began to laugh quietly to myself.

Uncle did indeed die on the third day, and in the few hours that preceded his passing he was extraordinarily lucid and loquacious. But his eyes were already piercing into other, different depths. Time and again he cried out: "Why have they taken away that painting by Mabuse? Charles Dideloo, you crook, put it back where it belongs! Nothing shall leave this house! Nothing! D'you hear me!"

Nancy came to calm him.

"Tell me, my lovely," he said, taking my sister's hands between his long, clawed paws, "tell me the names of those in this room here, because there are only shadows where there should be people . . ."

"The notary Schampe is sitting at the table with paper, pens, and an inkwell."

"Good. Schampe knows his job."

The notary, an old man of austere and honest countenance, greeted the dying man, although he was well aware Cassave could not see him.

"Who's sitting next to him?"

"There is only a vacant chair, Uncle."

"Have you summoned Eisengott, you she-devil?"

"Of course, Uncle. My brother Jean-Jacques is sitting next to you."

"Excellent. I'm pleased ... Ah! Jean-Jacques, my young friend, your grandfather was also my friend—and God, what a friend! He was a splendid rogue. He must be waiting for me now in some corner of eternity, which pleases me."

"The Misses Cormélon are here."

"Carrion attracts the crows! Well Elénore, Rosalie, and you too Alice—although you're the youngest and by a damned sight the prettiest—we've been on the best of terms now for a good long while. You understand me? Of course, *there are times when it is given to us to understand*, eh? Ugly you may be, but the Devil has put decent brains into your nasty heads. I owe you some of my last words and, since I imagine I owe you something else as well, I shall soon pay that debt."

"Cousin Philarète ..."

"He is my cousin. His blood is my own. He can't help it and what's more neither can I. He has every right to be here, although I'm inclined to think God Himself couldn't make a stupider man."

Philarète, too, bowed as if Uncle Cassave had been lauding him to the skies.

Cassave caught the gesture and smiled.

"Philarète was not a faithless servant," he said gently.

"Mathias Krook?" Nancy murmured after a brief hesitation.

Uncle Cassave seemed vexed.

"In excluding him from this company," he said, "I am possibly doing him an injustice. Well, he'll find consolation! So let him go back to the shop. He likes it there."

The old man had turned laboriously over onto his side to try to watch the youth go; I thought I could read in his expression a singular indecision.

"I've been mistaken in my time, Krook, not often, it's true, but I haven't the time now to mend my ways or undo my errors. Just or not—off you go!"

Mathias Krook disappeared from view, a miserable, shame-faced smile on his features; Nancy was looking daggers.

"Doctor Sambucus has just come in."

"Shove him in an armchair and give him something to nibble on."

"The Griboins are here."

"They were my good and faithful servants for more years than I care to add up. They will remain so."

"Lampernisse is sitting on the bottom step of the staircase; he's watching over a lamp that's still burning."

Uncle Cassave burst into a peal of sinister laughter.

"Let him stay there till it's blown out—and blown out it will be."

"Here are Uncle Charles Dideloo, Aunt Sylvie, and Euryale."

The dying man grimaced.

"There was a time when Sylvie was beautiful. She isn't any longer. I'm just as pleased not to see her. She was still beautiful when Uncle Charles came upon her at . . ."

"Great Uncle! Great Uncle!" Uncle Charles cried out in an anguished voice, "I implore you!"

"Go on then, Euryale, my lovely flower, go and sit down next to your cousin Jean-Jacques. You two are the double hope I take away with me from this earth."

A voice outside was begging: "No, no, don't put out the lamp!"

A man of imposing aspect entered and sat down beside the notary Schampe, without appearing to notice us.

"Eisengott is there!" Uncle Cassave cried.

"I have come," said a voice that rang like a bell.

I stared at the newcomer in terror and respect.

His face was very pale and very long, made longer still by an immense ashen beard that hung down, covering his chest like a waistcoat. His eyes were fixed and black, and his hands were so fine they seemed to have been borrowed from a recumbent figure on a church tomb. He was shabbily dressed and his green frock coat shone at the seams.

"Schampe!" said Uncle Cassave, "these people are my heirs. Tell them the total of the fortune I shall be leaving."

The notary bent over his papers and with deliberation pronounced a figure. It was so enormous, so formidable, so fantastic that for a moment we were all flabbergasted.

It was Aunt Sylvie who broke the spell cast by that golden number.

"Charles!" she exclaimed, "you shall hand in your notice!"

"Naturally," Uncle Cassave chuckled. "He couldn't do otherwise."

"This fortune," the notary declared, "is not to be divided among the co-owners."

A muttering of terrified disappointment arose; but the notary cut it short and continued.

"On the death of Quentin Moretus Cassave, all these persons here present, on pain of immediate exclusion from inheritance and loss of all future advantage, will live and continue to live under this roof."

"But we have a house, our own property," Elénore Cormélon wailed.

"Don't interrupt," the notary said severely. "They will live there until their death, but each will receive an annual income, that is to say a life annuity of..."

Once again the figure that fell from the notary's lips was prodigious.

I heard the eldest of the Cormélon sisters mumbling: "We'll sell the house."

"Each one of them will have the right of board and lodging, in respect of which the testator demands the best possible. The Griboin couple, whilst having the same advantages as the rest, will remain servants and will not forget this fact."

The notary paused.

"No changes will be made to the house of Malpertuis, and the entire fortune will be vested in the last survivor.

"The paint supplier's shop will be considered in the same terms as the house itself and Mathias Krook will remain the assistant, his wages tripled and guaranteed for life. Only the last survivor will have the right to close the said shop.

"Eisengott, who shall derive no advantage, to whom nothing is due, and who wants nothing, shall oversee the perfect execution of these wishes."

The notary turned to the last page of the document.

"There follows a codicil: If the last two survivors be a man and a woman, the Dideloo couple being *de facto* excluded, they shall become man and wife and the fortune shall revert to them in equal parts."

A silence hung over the company; they had not yet taken in what had been disclosed.

"Such are my wishes!" Uncle Cassave said in a firm tone.

"And so it shall be," the somber Eisengott responded gravely.

"Sign!" the notary Schampe commanded.

They all signed. Cousin Philarète put a cross.

"Be off with you!" said Uncle Cassave, whose face had suddenly become drawn. "Eisengott, you will remain."

We retired to the dimness of the yellow drawing room.

"Who will be meeting the cost of our move here?" the elder Cormélon asked.

"I will," Nancy declared.

"And why *you*, Mademoiselle?"

"Would you like me to have Eisengott tell you?" my sister inquired quietly.

"It seems to me . . ." Uncle Charles broke in.

"Never mind what it seems to you!" Nancy exploded. "In any case, here's Monsieur Eisengott."

He walked to the center of the room, brooding over us with his terrible and somber gaze.

"Monsieur Cassave wishes Jean-Jacques and Euryale to help him in his last moments."

Every head was bowed, even Nancy's.

Uncle Cassave was barely breathing, and his eyes reflected the light like glass marbles.

"In your chair, Jean-Jacques . . . Sit in your chair . . . and you, Euryale, come close to me."

My cousin slipped gracefully over to him, obedient but oddly indifferent to the strange majesty of the moment.

"Open your eyes, daughter of the gods," my uncle murmured in a voice that was utterly changed and which seemed to have in it a terrified respect. "Open your eyes and help me die . . ."

Euryale bent over him.

He gave a long, drawn-out sigh, and I heard a few words escape him and dissolve into the silence.

"My heart in Malpertuis . . . a stone among the stones . . ."

My cousin remained motionless for so long that I took fright.

"Euryale . . ." I pleaded.

She turned to me, a singular smile on her lips. From beneath her half-closed eyelids there filtered only a distant stare, lacking life and thought.

"Uncle is dead," she said.

And then a prolonged lamentation broke out on the stairs.

"He's blown out the lamp . . . I was watching, watching so closely, and yet he put it out. Oh, it's gone out!"

2

Malpertuis Described

The genie of the night bore off the fox's head wherewith to adorn his house and do it honor.

—The Tales of Hussein[9]

The sun! Give me the sun!

—Ibsen, *Ghosts*[10]

The lesser gods, such as the penates, the brownies or the Glasmännchen, are never spirits but minuscule incarnations and thus absolutely material, and draw their power from the earth in which they live.

—Worth, *Comparative Folklore*[11]

Now that I must describe Malpertuis I find myself stricken with a strange impotence. The image recedes like the castles of Morgan le Fay;[12] the brush becomes like lead in the painter's head; so many things I would like to fix by description or definition vanish, become vague, and dissolve into misty nothingness.

Were it not for my excellent teacher, the Abbé Doucedame, who often obliged me to see rather than merely look, I should have turned aside from the task.

Six weeks before Uncle Cassave died, we had left our house on the Quai de la Balise for Malpertuis.

The house on the Quai will remain sweet in my memory. It was small and strangely constructed; its green-glass windows bathed it in an aquarium light of infinite gentleness; it smelled of verbena and tobacco—the tobacco the Abbé Doucedame, a regular guest, smoked.

The door opened onto a hall, the one spacious place under that narrow roof, a hall watched over by the portrait of my father, Captain Nicolas Grandsire, guarded in its turn by fearsome suits of armor.

The Captain used to send us sufficient money to meet the rent and to permit us to live without undue worry. But toward the time when Uncle Cassave summoned us, the checks on the banks of Singapore, Shanghai, or Canton had become increasingly meager and infrequent.

In the days of our relative prosperity Elodie had kept open house to certain friends, and the Abbé Doucedame was the most respected among them, as well as the most assiduous.

He was a small man, plump and rotund as a hogshead, with a cheerful full-moon face and a greasy soutane.

He loved good cooking—and Elodie's cooking was of the first order—reputable wines, Dutch tobacco, and old books.

His name has not been engulfed in oblivion, and rightly not, for it is associated with certain publications that still retain a degree of authority. Thus we are indebted to him for an elaborate study of the engravings of Wendel Dietterlin, a most original biography of Gerrit Dou, and research into the artistic ironwork of the fifteenth century.[13]

He continued the curious studies of Doctor Mises of Leipzig concerning the forms, the language, and the comparative anatomy of angels.[14]

He held that these celestial spirits express their thoughts by means of light and that to this end they make use of colors instead of sounds.

He regularly said his office, never shirked a moment of his breviary, and lived a life of exemplary chastity and humility, but this did little to endear him to his superiors. His having resumed Doctor Mises's studies had, in effect, won him an unwarranted reputation as a heretic and even a few punitive retreats in especially austere monasteries. But the youth of that priest had been spent in distant and dangerous climes, where the glory of God is defended at the cost of the suffering and the blood of the soldiers of Christ— and even meddlesome and whining bishops did not dare deny it.

Had Doucedame come to know Captain Nicolas Grandsire in the course of those perilous adventures? He never said anything himself on that score, and my father contented himself with concluding his letters: *kindest regards to the saintly Tatou. May god protect him for the sake of the happiness of the poor in this life and for their access to eternal glory.*

"What's a tatou?" Elodie would ask suspiciously.

"It's a fat beast—like myself," the Abbé Doucedame would explain. "However, it has remained on the banks of the Amazon— which I haven't done, seeing as I'm here to drink good wine and eat good things, and ill deserve divine mercy."

"How," I asked him, pretending to take notes, "do you explain the name of Malpertuis, which Uncle Cassave's house seems to bear as if it were a curse?"

Before giving an explanation, the Abbé Doucedame assumed an incongruous air of grave attention.

"In the celebrated and uncourtly *Roman de Renart* the clerics gave that name to the lair of the cunning and evil fox, Goupil. I would not wish to venture an opinion as to whether Malpertuis means the house of evil or the house of *malitia*, of cunning. Now *malitia*, cunning, is the prerogative of the Spirit of Darkness. By extension of the postulate thus posed, I would say that it means *la maison du Malin*, the house of the Devil . . ."[15]

I made a grimace of fear.

"My own personal inclination, however, is for 'the fox,' pure and simple. On the lintels of the double windows of the facade there are some disagreeable carvings . . .

"Arrowhead squids, heraldic serpents devouring babes, herpetons," itemized the Abbé.[16]

"And among those carvings, the foxes' heads are the pleasantest; the stone corbels of the projecting beams bear the same motifs."

"They're wicked looking, big-eared dogs and nothing more. But don't jump to conclusions, my young friend, don't jump to conclusions. The representation of the fox belongs by right to demonology. The Japanese, who are masters of that somber and dreaded science, have made the fox a sorcerer, a mighty thaumaturge, and a nocturnal spirit gifted with the most extensive infernal powers. I've seen seven grimoires—the reading of which, much less the *knowledge* of which, I must condemn without mercy—in which the engravings representing the battle between Saint Michael and the rebellious angel give the defeated Evil One the mean and perverse aspect of the fox.

"Unfortunately, the archives—and I have consulted them time and time again—have not revealed to me the reason for the choice of this name for Uncle Cassave's house. I believe we owe it to the

Barbusquin monks, owners in past times of the principal outbuildings of that dwelling—which I find dismal and menacing."

"Tell me about the Barbusquin order," I said abruptly, knowing perfectly well that he was disinclined to touch upon the subject.

With his plump little arms he would gesture his helplessness and vexation.

"That order . . . that order . . . Oh, come now, my boy! The fact is it never existed; the denomination is merely popular.

"The good monks of whom you would speak were reformed Cistercians who suffered greatly from the depredations of vagabonds, by land and sea, in the times of the great revolt of the Netherlands against His Catholic Majesty . . ."

Nonetheless I persisted.

"Perhaps your monks had beards . . ."

"No, no. You're falling into a popular delusion. Those monks wore a *barbute*, a cowl that enveloped their chins—and so, too, their beards—and it is there perhaps that the reason for their name is to be found. But I do not go so far as to assert this, still less to commit it to writing. Let us leave the dead in peace, especially when they were holy men of many virtues born of suffering and persecution."

"Aha, Abbé! I have a feeling tradition will decide quite differently!"

"Be quiet!" the Abbé Doucedame implored. "Tradition is a detestable peddler of errors, to which, alas, the Devil lends a long and tenacious life."

After setting down this conversation, which was not unique but repeated on a number of occasions in a similar manner, I feel better prepared to resume the description of Malpertuis.

I have often pored over ancient engravings of the town, portraying old streets heavy with boredom and disdain, streets resistant to every effort to animate them with life and movement.

Among these I had no trouble in finding the Rue du Vieux Chantier where Malpertuis is situated and, without undue trouble, I made out the house itself, set amongst its tall and sinister neighbors.

There it stands with its enormous pillared balconies, its flights of steps flanked with heavy stone banisters, its cruciferous turrets, its gemel barred windows, its grimacing, sculptured child-eating serpents and tarasques,[17] its studded doors.

It exudes the arrogance of its inhabitants and the terror of those who skirt its outer walls.

Its facade is a severe mask in which the beholder vainly seeks any serenity, a face feverishly twisted in rage and anguish that fails to conceal the abominations that lie behind it. Those who lie down to sleep in its vast rooms lay themselves open to nightmares; those who spend their days there are obliged to habituate themselves to the company of the atrocious shades of executed criminals, of men flayed alive, or walled up, or otherwise tormented.

Such must have been the unbidden thoughts of the passerby who halts awhile in its shadow—and who immediately makes off to the end of the road where there are a few trees, a murmuring fountain, a white stone dovecote, and a chapel dedicated to Our Lady of the Seven Sorrows.

Alas, that is what turns me abruptly away from my project!

The Abbé Doucedame put into words everything that the old archives might have been able to tell of that house—but which they did not tell.

I have entered Malpertuis. I belong to it. It makes no mystery of its interior. There is no door that insists upon remaining closed, no room that balks at my curiosity; there is no forbidden chamber, no secret passage; and yet . . .

And yet at every exploratory step it contrives to remain mysterious, and at every exploratory step it continues to encompass a shifting prison of shadows.

The Abbé Doucedame has sometimes manifested a certain curiosity concerning its garden, which is as extensive as a park and surrounded by a wall so high, so formidable, that it is only toward midday that the sun projects the shadow of its ragged crest.

When one leans out of the upper windows of the house and looks down, the garden is like a broad, flat, grassy expanse from which centuries-old trees burst like water spouts; in fact, the grass is sparse and coarse; the spindle bushes are skimpy and the brushwood has an undernourished look; only the wild oats and the dock triumph over the ungrateful soil and sprout rankly at the base of the walls.

The trees mount a jealous guard against the daylight and appear to be accommodating to all manner of larval life and a flourishing lushness of cryptogams.

But such life as one might expect to find among trees remained exiled from that place; it is in vain that one might seek the jaunty swaggering of blackbirds, the timid flight of ring doves, the bickering of jays.

Once, at midnight, I heard the thin song of the woodlark, that mysterious lark of darkness—and the Abbé Doucedame saw in this a sign of misfortune and menace.

There is, though, a long-legged water rail that lives among the *sagittaria* in the central pond and, now and again, its squealing note, like a file on metal, can be heard; in foggy weather the dotterels' weeping call comes trickling from the depths of the heavens.

This pond, which is of some size, opens up suddenly on the far side of a barrier of stunted oaks that stand crowded together, their short, gnarled branches intertwined.

The inky blackness of the waters betray their enormous depth; they are so icily cold as to seem to bite the hand plunged into them. Despite this they are well provided with fish and Griboin catches mirror carp, gleaming perch, and great bluish eels there in a Garonne bow-net—one of the kind called a *bergot*. Some forty yards from the southern bank of the pond is a second hedge, this one of tall and gloomy conifers, so rebarbative that one hesitates to pass it.

Once past this gloom-enshrouded and prickly barrier, one finds oneself facing a building of improbable ugliness, its stones blighted, rotted as if with leprosy, its windows broken, its roof gaping: the ruins of the ancient monastery of the Barbusquins.

A gigantic flight of high stone steps leads up to the iron-bound door.

My good Abbé Doucedame needed to pluck up his courage before climbing those steps and then give himself over to the exploration of those miserable quarters, so well defended by their hideousness.

He had proposed devoting a short book to the ruins; in the event he took some ill-ordered and wildly excited notes, but he never put together the little work from which he nonetheless had counted upon deriving some fame. *I am amazed,* he wrote, *at the discomfort in which the good monks lived here, and I would go so far as to claim that they sought herein a means of holy penitence. The cells are cramped with low ceilings; they are poorly lit and ventilated. The tables and benches and the refectory are of coarse gray stone. The chapel is so dark and lofty as to be like a well. Nowhere (the vast and forbidding kitchens excepted) is there any trace of fires or fireplaces. Part of the cellars would appear to have been fitted out as laboratories, for one still finds there massive flues, a brickwork alembic of considerable proportions, water conduits, and the troughs of forges. In days gone by the learned monks may perhaps at times have become addicted to spagyria,*[18] *even though the practice was condemned.*

Likewise I cannot but be surprised at the unusual extent of the cellars, now unexplorable as a consequence of collapses in parts of the ceiling, partial flooding, and patches of ruderal vegetation that might be of interest to an informed botanist. It is evident that the epoch, sadly rich in persecutions, obliged the good monks to provide themselves with this species of retreat and the means of communication or flight.

I should have liked to have handed over to the Abbé the exploration—manifestly the softer option—of the house itself; but this he refused with an obstinacy that sometimes bordered on the ill-tempered.

On the rare occasions on which he put in an appearance there he would remain huddled in his chair, his head bowed, his lips compressed, his hands damp and trembling and, during the long intervals of silence that ensued on such visits, I suspect him of having muttered complicated exorcisms. No doubt God, whose humble servant he was, had vouchsafed him a glimpse of the dreadful fate reserved for that fearful house, which he accepted as the saints accept martyrdom.

Only the lugubrious kitchen found favor in his terrified eyes; Elodie played her part in his tolerating, perhaps even challenging other presences, which were occult, invisible, but nonetheless formidable.

The poor, dear man's besetting sin was the deadly sin of gluttony; he would sigh deeply when faced with *soufflés à la moelle,*[19] gigots of lamb fragrant with garlic, or the streamingly rich fowl our cook would set before him on the gleaming oaken table.

His soul tormented with remorse, he would pick with his fork at the over-rich delicacies, cutting into fillets, crushing the stewed fruits; and as he ate his sauce-bedewed lips would attempt a vague smile, intended to be sour and woebegone, but which would by degrees modulate into one of happy contentment.

In the long run he managed to convince himself of the innocence of his greedy pleasures.

"If God has scattered the quiet hollows of the meadows with mushrooms, if He has placed a fleshy comb on the cock's peaked skull, if He has caused the wild garlic to flourish in sheltered valleys and permitted the Madeira grape to ripen in southern regions, His aim was not to make salami—whose flavor they enhance—an agent of damnation. In any case they ate poorly at the table of Minos . . ."

So he went on; but he would shudder if he mentioned the name of the Prince of Darkness and a faint anxiety would trouble his frank, blue-eyed gaze.

I frequently raised questions that troubled the good Abbé, especially when they touched on Malpertuis, on Uncle Cassave, and indeed on my father, Nicolas Grandsire.

He would pontificate at such moments: "There are books," he would insist, "in which once one has read a page, one cannot turn back. Life is afflicted with a chronic crick in the neck, which prevents one from ever taking a backward glance. Let us do likewise. The past belongs to death, and death keeps a watchful eye on what belongs to him."

"Death had to relinquish Lazarus," I would reply.

"*Will* you hold your tongue, you young wretch!"

"But Lazarus hadn't much to say for himself . . . Ah! if only he'd been able to leave us his memoirs!"

And the Abbé Doucedame would get annoyed.

"The way you express yourself, without either consideration or respect, involves me in thoroughly unpleasant supplementary penances," he used to complain.

Taking leave of him on the threshold of Malpertuis I used sometimes to restrain him, laying hold of the tails of his old soutane.

"Why did Uncle Cassave buy a shop?"

I would accompany him into the street and oblige him to turn and face the oddly coupled pair of facades—that of the proud house and the strange shop with its lusterless windows.

It was a narrow building, without architectural distinction, although it dated from the times when art and harmony were the rule.

Its high, pointed gable, surmounted by a weathercock and a sandstone turret, leaned backwards, as if it had received a brutal blow; its windows were hardly more than double loopholes with bottle-green panes that, at first sight, gleamed as if waxed.

The old sign still hung over the door: *Lampernisse, Couleurs et Vernis.*

"Why?" I would insist. "Why? Nancy and Mathias Krook spend their days there and they never do five francs' worth of business."

In replying the Abbé would sometimes assume an air of mystery.

"Colors ... Ah, my poor, dear boy, you should remember the magnificent studies of Doctor Mises. Colors ... the words of angels ... Uncle Cassave wished to steal something from our celestial friends. But hush! It isn't good to speak of these things; one never knows what entities are on the alert to hear our words and our thoughts."

With an abrupt movement he would disengage his soutane and make off, without looking back; on windy days the tempest would whip up his coattails, making them look like great black wings.

My dear Elodie was a simple but sensible woman.

"God keeps His own council and punishes those men who seek to cast a profane slur upon it," she would reply to my idle words. "Why shouldn't the Devil, who apes all things that are God's, wish to do as much? Be content, Jean-Jacques, to live according to His law, to renounce the Devil and all his works, to say your rosary daily and piously. It is also good to wear a scapular and call upon the names of certain meritorious saints."

And no doubt she was right … If, as we shall see, the tide of horror had thundered about Elodie as it did about others, the gloomy spell of Malpertuis would not have been able directly to assail her.

The ceremonial installation—I openly admit the expression is a trifle high flown—of the new inhabitants of Malpertuis took place without undue disturbances or difficulties.

Cousin Philarète was by a comfortable margin the first to arrive, his scanty effects piled on a handcart he pushed himself.

Nancy had reserved for him a vast room overlooking the garden, with which he immediately declared himself well satisfied; within a couple of hours it reeked of formaldehyde, iodoform, and spirits of wine.

He loaded the table with cupules, brain extractors, tweezers, balls of cotton wool, saucers filled with glass eyes and coloring powders. A lifeless but startlingly lifelike fauna loomed on all sides, on the shelves and on the furniture, encompassing the bejeweled azure of the kingfisher and the black elegance of the sand martin, ranging from the wary look of a silvery weasel to the snarling defiance of an Australian lizard, from the velvety softness of red-breasted mergansers to the livid emaciation of reptiles.

"Cousin Jean-Jacques," Philarète proposed, "we really ought to come to an arrangement. In a big garden like that, you ought to be able to catch me plenty of beasts—furred or feathered, it doesn't much matter which. I could turn them out for you even prettier than if they were alive."

"All I've ever seen is a scruffy water-rail," I replied unenthusiastically.

"Get him! Get him for me, and you'll see whether he'll turn out as nasty a bird as you say he is!"

The Dideloo family arrived without any fuss.

When I came upon them in the roomy first-floor apartment Nancy had ungrudgingly set aside for them, Aunt Sylvie was already at work embroidering a bulky blue canvas and Uncle Charles was rehanging a picture. My cousin Euryale had retired to her own room and did not deign to put in an appearance.

As might have been expected, the Misses Cormélon proved to be less accommodating. True, my sister had relegated them to a suite of rooms at the end of an echoing, stone-flagged passage, so lofty as to be like so many chapels; but they criticized everything, and even the fine Gobelin tapestries on the walls found no favor in their eyes.

"The creatures in them are enough to give you nightmares," they complained.

"We'll need every bit of thirty candles to light each of those rooms properly," Eléonore declared firmly.

Nancy's reply was sharp and apt.

"There are six to a room; but seeing that Schampe has provided the first monthly payment in advance, you're well able to provide the other two dozen yourselves."

"We'll spend *our* money as we see fit," was the shrill response, "and in this matter we can manage without your advice."

Doctor Sambucus was awarded a strange and quite amusing room, completely round in shape, part of a tower flanking the west wing of the house. He found it to his taste, preferring, so he said, the splendid mellowness of sunsets to the insolent ardor of dawns.

Nancy encountered Lampernisse as he was pouring oil into one of the lamps in the hallway; she offered him a little room, quite well lit and comfortable, in the south annex.

He refused it angrily.

"No, no!—I don't want it . . . O goddess . . . *He* must not know where I live. I hide where *He* cannot find me and steal the light and the colors!"

As always, Nancy smiled; and he decamped, wailing.

The dining room where the inhabitants were compelled to gather twice daily, for lunch at midday and for supper at seven, was vast and it was certainly the only sumptuous room in that grim dwelling.

The dark wooden furniture, inlaid with ebony and rosy mother-of-pearl, took on in the light of the lamps and the tall, twisted candles the gleaming depths of gems of the first water; cascades of aventurines streamed in the space where the midday sun's beams pierced the stained-glass windows.

A hearth of unusual dimensions looked something like a house fire once the logs were lit; it was flanked by andirons and solid silver firedogs.

The Griboin couple, willingly helped by Elodie, served at table and, in keeping with the will of the late Uncle Cassave, every meal there was like a banquet.

Although the table companions gave the impression of having come together with the plain intention of showing themselves to be as formal and as nicely spoken as possible, I admit that the first meal was almost diverting.

The Misses Cormélon ate enough for four, asking for second helpings of everything, with the sole purpose of consuming as much as possible of what was theirs by right.

Aunt Sylvie, having simpered with regret before the hors-d'oeuvres, bravely attacked the roast and guzzled with a will, greasing her table napkin and splashing the cloth.

Uncle Dideloo quickly came to appreciate the rare quality of the wines—and his lecherous regard lingered over my sister's abundantly rounded forms.

Doctor Sambucus, seated next to Cousin Philarète, immediately hit it off with him.

"Ah! mmm! mmm!" the taxidermist warbled in his voracious enthusiasm, "I don't know what this is I'm eating, but it's devilish good!"

"It's a *filet au porto à la purée de noisettes*,"[20] the old doctor explained.

"I wonder if they couldn't have it again tomorrow?" Philarète asked, nudging him with his elbow.

He took great pleasure in admiring the little figures decorating the wonderful Moustiers plates on which the *riz au rhum*[21] was served with fresh cream.

"There's a devil with six horns on mine!" he exclaimed. "How about yours, Doctor? . . . Aha! A fellow drinking from a barrel!"

He tried to look at the others' plates, to the great annoyance of the Misses Cormélon who covered theirs with their table napkins while asking Cousin Philarète whether he had any acquaintance at all with good society.

The poor fellow failed to see any malice at all in their inquiry and answered that he had undoubtedly just made his entry into the very best of society.

Nancy, who was not at heart an unpleasant girl, seemed to take a real pleasure in the first breaking of the ice; but I felt rather at a loss as regards Euryale.

She sat stiff and upright in her chair, eating little and that with a manifest displeasure. Her eyes, peering abstractly into vacancy, were lusterless and even when, by chance, they fell on me, I had the impression she did not see me.

She was wearing a wretched little dress of uncertain color; it was too tight and flattened her figure; but at the least movement of her head her awe-inspiring tresses were illuminated in glowing red glints and were as if alive.

Once the table was cleared, Uncle Charles proposed they amuse themselves.

To my amazement, the Misses Cormélon opted for a game of whist, with Uncle as fourth.

Cousin Philarète chortled with delight when Doctor Sambucus challenged him to a game of checkers.

Aunt Sylvie curled up in an armchair and went to sleep. To Uncle Dideloo's obvious disappointment Nancy precipitately vanished. Without my being aware of her coming, Euryale appeared at my side. I experienced a strange, almost painful sensation at the back of my neck: she had placed her hand there, and her fingers were hard and cold. They remained there so long, so long that I felt as if my being were freezing into eternity.

The crystalline notes of a wall clock sounded eleven.

The Misses Cormélon were clucking with pleasure: Uncle Dideloo had lost a couple of francs.

"You're a much better player than I'd thought, Philarète," said Doctor Sambucus with a touch of regret.

"I regularly play checkers at the *Petit Marquis*," the taxidermist excused himself, "but Piekenbot the cobbler often beats me."

"You'll have to learn chess," Sambucus proclaimed.

Aunt Sylvie woke up yawning. Gold gleamed in her mouth.

"Jean-Jacques . . . ," Euryale murmured.

"What? . . . what's that . . . ?" I replied quietly, but with a considerable effort, for a strange torpor had been weighing me down ever since she had rested her hand on the back of my neck.

"Listen to me, but don't say anything."

"Of course, Euryale."

"When all these people are dead, except ourselves, you will marry me . . ."

I should've liked to have turned and looked at her, but her hand grew still heavier and colder upon me, and I could not make the slightest movement. But a pier glass facing us reflected our images.

In it I saw two green, immobile flames burning, like two enormous moonstones in the depths of a nocturnal lake.

3

The Song of Songs

I saw the Capitano, his head nailed to the mast, and I realized that he had just been struck down by the gods.
    —Wilhelm Hauff, *The Phantom Ship*[22]

The autumn came and went, spreading neither joy nor glory over the town. It is possible that beyond the ramparts it gilded the woods, that it padded the rutted tracks with soft heaps of leaves, easy underfoot, that it drew the hymn of its fecundity from the harp of the orchards and scattered generous handfuls of sane and healthy pleasures; but once within the city limits it showed itself sparing in its largesse and its smiles.

The facades of the houses wept, saturated with deep sorrows; the streets were filled with the sharp sound of running water; a phantom hand impatiently rattled every door, every window, at the mercy of the gusting winds.

Isolated on the embankments, the trees were no more than skeletal charcoal sketches and the dead leaves, carried on the wind, lashed at the faces of passersby.

The chimneys of Malpertuis, adorned with armorial bearings, belched forth heavy columns of smoke into the gray air, for in every room a vast fire of logs and coal was roaring.

When the silvery note of the wall clocks struck four, when the insistent scent of coffee rose from the kitchens, the Griboins would hasten about the house bearing lighted lamps which they set down in their usual positions—at the angles of corridors, on landings, in niches in the hall.

Malpertuis never seemed more somber than when spangled with these remote and smoky stars.

At these times the distant prospect of the paint suppliers' shop, which could be glimpsed at the far end of one of the lateral corridors of the ground floor, assumed the reassuring air of a haven of light. I would often have made my way in that direction, had I not met with the silent hostility of Nancy and Mathias Krook.

The shop was their domain and they made it plain that they had no intention of sharing its advantages with anybody.

At times a shadow huddled on a staircase would sob and sigh as I passed: it was Lampernisse who, from afar, kept watch over this lost paradise.

I should've liked to become his friend, for he inspired in me a strange pity and even a kind of confused affection, but he avoided me, just as he fled the presence of each and all of us. I persisted, however, seeking to surprise him on his rounds and exchange with him a few brief, friendly words.

I was to some extent recompensed for this persistence—if the first harrowing discovery I made in Malpertuis, thanks to Lampernisse, might be called a recompense.

The first phantom to rise up before me was that common to all sequestered lives: *ennui*.

Day in, day out, it rained, and at certain times the downpour would take on the character of a raging deluge.

There was no counting upon the garden and its repulsive mysteries to distract myself from the dismal and silent hours I spent in the house. The leafless branches of the trees clashed together; the rain-lashed earth erupted into blisters and pustules that broke and dissolved into mud; during the brief spells of respite, when the branches and the twigs as it were drew breath, one could hear the surly lapping sound of the waters of the pond.

The house possessed a well-stocked library, but I am no great reader; in any case the books, bound in somber leather, smelled of moldy boots.

When I did once venture a visit there, I found Uncle Dideloo and Alice, the youngest of the Cormélon sisters, already in possession.

I was aware of gestures of embarrassment, and my uncle attempted to get on his high horse.

"A well-educated young man never enters a room without knocking!"

"I'm not a well-educated young man," I retorted. "And it's not as if I expected to find anything here but mice!"

I slammed the door behind me as I left, after the manner of Nancy; and I reflected that Alice Cormélon was not, when it came to the point, particularly ugly.

Thereafter Uncle Dideloo treated me very coolly, but the youngest Cormélon sister would cast looks in my direction in which anxiety was blended with a vague smile of complicity.

I still found a refuge with Elodie; nevertheless, at those times when her stoves did not demand her attention, she was absorbed in her rosary and her prayer book.

"We must say a prayer to Saint Vénérande, asking her to intercede for a change in the weather, so we can have a bit of sun and you can go and amuse yourself in the garden.

Noble et sainte Vénérande,
À vous je fais humble offrande . . ."[23]

I have no idea what it was that I was humbly offering Saint Vénérande; I left the kitchen well before the end of the pious evocation and went in search of refuge with Cousin Philarète.

If it were not for the heavy atmosphere of the room, I think I might have found a fairly lasting diversion there; but the almost visible odor of carbolic that hung in the place made me retch.

The taxidermist was always working on some disgusting treasure, the sickening evolution of which he loved to show me.

"You must bring me animals, my boy. I haven't got many and, to tell the truth, I find it difficult to get hold of them here. When it stops raining, couldn't you give a thought to that water rail that lives in the garden?"

One day there was a new smell among the mingled fetors.

"Ah, Cousin Philarète!" I blurted out, "I've never seen you smoke!"

"I don't smoke, Cousin Jean-Jacques."

"All the same, there's a smell of tobacco—and good tobacco too!"

"It's the Abbé Doucedame who smokes, not me."

"What's that?" I exclaimed in astonishment. "The Abbé Doucedame comes here?"

"He came here," Philarète replied curtly, "and he snubbed me."

I was not just surprised but also hurt to hear that my excellent teacher had come to Malpertuis without my knowledge.

I shall say nothing of Elénore and Rosalie Cormélon, whose company I avoided and who certainly had no wish for mine.

As for the Griboins, their concierge's lodge was as joyless as their persons. When I chanced to enter, those too polite and faithful servants afforded me the welcome reserved for a stranger whose coming is neither expected nor desired. They would inquire after my health, comment on the day's weather and on yesterday's and predict tomorrow's, bidding me on my departure an effusive farewell.

Things were no different with Aunt Sylvie, who adopted during my visits to her personal sitting room the silence and immobility of a statue; nor, alas, with Euryale—Euryale, whom I desired with the feverish intensity of a treasure hunter and who, outside of the hours we took our meals together, would vanish like a shadow; whom I never saw rounding the corner of a corridor, who never appeared in a doorway, whom one never expected to find seated in one of the drawing rooms, who never leaned out of a half-open window. Ennui flitted about me on its shabby bats' wings; and it was ennui that drove me to seek out the incomprehensible, phantasmal, clownish figure so strangely haunted by the shadow of his shadow: Lampernisse.

One day Cousin Philarète drew me aside.

"I've made a new mousetrap. It's a fine piece of work, big and roomy, and it doesn't kill or injure the animals it catches. You know the house, Cousin; you must set it for me, in a good place—in the attics, for example."

"You'd only catch mice or rats."

"No doubt, no doubt—but who ever knows? Those old attics are a world all to themselves. I remember a certain Monsieur Likkendorf who lived in the neighborhood of the docks and who caught a magnificent pink rat in a trap—an unknown species. And my friend Piekenbot, the cobbler, told me that in his mother's attics there are mice with trunks. And then again . . ."

Doctor Sambucus called out to my interlocutor.

"Hey there, Philarète—come and have your chess lesson!"

The taxidermist thrust a bulky cage trap into my hands, its hooks baited with chunks of bacon and leftover ends of cheese.

"Good hunting, Cousin! . . . You never know, eh?"

In itself the matter aroused no interest in me, but the idea of exploring the attics of Malpertuis promised an antidote to my boredom.

I climbed endless stairs, some so broad and majestic as to seem to give access to temple halls, others twisting and narrow and precipitous spirals to end in trapdoors I was obliged to force with my shoulders.

And abruptly I was there.

The place was made up of a succession of deeply indented polyhedra, picked out by the gray light of the dormer windows and œils-de-bœuf. It was completely empty; no rocking chair lurked there, relegated to an obscure corner; no outmoded chest leaned against the walls of tarnished bricks to avoid falling into dust; no set of worm-eaten suitcases was laid out on the floor, which was flush as the deck of a packet boat.

It was cold, and the wind, whistling over the roof tiles, filled the emptiness there with its sighs and caterwauling.

I threw the trap down any old how and beat a retreat, resolving to limit the services I rendered to Cousin Philarète to that one brief intrusion into the heights of Malpertuis.

Two days went by.

I was awakened that morning earlier than usual by a gust of wind so violent that it all but burst open the French window of my room. In the wan light of a sinister dawn, tinted—or tainted—with the lemon-yellow gleams of the rising sun, I caught sight of the garden tormented by the howling fury of a ferocious downpour of rain.

I was shivering: a humid chill had crept like a snake under the sheets. At that hour, I thought, Elodie must already be lighting the fires in the kitchen; it would be warm and pleasant there.

I hastily left my room.

A pallid light was playing over the corridors where the dead and dying lamps trailed a thick stench of cooling oil and burnt-out wicks.

I had reached the hall on the ground floor which led to the kitchen stairs when, suddenly, through the banisters, a livid hand grasped me by the shoulder.

I let out a cry.

"Shhh! Shhh! don't call anybody . . . they mustn't know," a pitiful voice pleaded.

I found myself face to face with Lampernisse.

He was trembling in every limb, and his fleshless silhouette was shuddering like a storm-tossed bush.

"It was you, wasn't it, that set the trap?" he sobbed. "So you know, then? . . . I'd never have dared . . . Well . . . one of them's been caught!! Come and see. I'd never dare to go there on my own. I'll keep behind you, well behind you. Do you think it's they who put out the lamps?"

It was useless to oppose the old man. His hand gripped my arm like a vice and he drew me up the staircase at an amazing pace.

I remade the ascent of the day before last, this time at a disconcerting velocity, for Lampernisse was literally carrying me with him.

Never could he have been more loquacious than in those febrile moments, nor happier, for amid the filthy growth that sprouted from his features his eyes were burning with a fiery joy.

He drew closer to me with an air of mystery, as if to impart a grave confidence.

"I know in my heart *He's* the one ... But why can't *He* forget too, and at the same time forget *me*? Time and the powers here are subject to strange whims that impose on one, by turns, forgetfulness and memory. Suppose *He* had forgotten and it was *they* who put out the lamps? I think I know them. They're so angry at being small they mimic anyone large. But they didn't count among those who play a role in the workings of fate; no task was assigned to them. Now they can be caught in a miserable rattrap! Aha! It'd serve them right! I'll kill them, I'll torture them, and keep my lamps lit, without anybody daring to rob me of my colors!"

"I don't know what you're talking about, Lampernisse," I said gently, "nor do I understand you."

"Ah!" he said, "in this place that's all anyone can say."

His wild high spirits diminished as we reached the final flights of the narrow spiral stairs leading to the attics.

"Wait a moment," he murmured. "Do you hear something?"

He was trembling so violently that his shuddering was communicated to my body like the abrupt discharges of a Leyden jar.

And indeed, I did hear something ...

It was a fine, sharp sound, drilling into the eardrums; the sound of a minuscule file, wielded frantically.

From time to time it was briefly silenced; during these short silences the enraged chirping of birds could be heard.

"My God!" Lampernisse was sobbing, "*THEY* are letting him loose!"

I rebuffed him jeeringly.

"Since when did rats make use of files to get their friends out of traps?"

The old man's livid claws closed on me like the talons of a bird of prey.

"Don't say another word . . . And above all don't open the trapdoor, otherwise they'll be all over the house! There'll never be light again! You understand, you wretch? No lamps, no sun, no moon . . . It'll be the eternal night of damnation. Let's be off!"

On the far side of the trapdoor I heard a sharp, snapping sound, as if of a stick breaking, a harsh cry, and then laughter.

Oh, that laughter! It was not loud, but so harsh it seemed made of forceps and scalpels . . .

I struggled in Lampernisse's grip and, with the help of a sly and well-placed kick that drew from him a yelp of pain, I freed myself.

"I want to see!" I roared.

The old man emitted a wild, raucous bellowing sound and fell away; a moment later I heard him racing blindly down the stairs uttering dismal lamentations.

It was now quite silent behind the trap door.

I pushed it up with my shoulders.

The pale, glimmering light of dawn was filtering through the dormer windows; a few feet from me lay the broken trap.

I lifted it in fear and disgust: a red bead was shining feebly on the little slat of smoothed boxwood, a teardrop of fresh blood.

And, an inch away from it, gripping one of the baits . . .

A hand.

A neatly severed hand, the cut showing clean and pink.

A perfect hand, its skin fine and brown, the size of ... a housefly.

But from each finger of that ghastly miniature hand there grew a nail, sharply pointed as a needle and inordinately long. I threw the trap and its hideous wonder as far as I could from me, into the darkest corner of the loft.

It was still night in that ill-lit attic, where the dawn light had hardly penetrated, and in that half-light I saw ...

I saw something the size of which barely exceeded that of an ordinary rat ...

It was a being of human form, but hideously dwarfish. Behind it other creatures, identical in all points, were massed together. They were grotesques, shameless, insect-like parodies of the being made in the divine image. And these creatures, minuscule as they were, were the very expression of horror, rage, and menace.

Anticipating an attack by these minute monstrosities, I let loose a piercing cry, and my retreat was every bit as precipitate as that of Lampernisse; I fell headlong down the narrow, winding stairs, leapt down the staircases a flight at a time, and shot like an arrow along the landings.

It was then that I saw Lampernisse again.

He was galloping through the corridors, brandishing a torch that trailed a long red tongue of flame. He was rushing from lamp to lamp, touching the flame to each wick, awakening discs of golden light in the darkness.

Powerless and terrified, I watched his vain struggle against the darkness of Malpertuis.

Hardly had he kindled into existence the flame of a lamp than a swift shadow detached itself from the wall, fell on the light, and extinguished it, reestablishing the darkness.

And then Lampernisse screamed: the torch was dead in his hand.

～✕

In the days that followed I saw nothing of Lampernisse although, in the hours of darkness, I could hear him, as always, coming and going—and sobbing.

Cousin Philarète said nothing further to me about his trap, and I for my part took good care not to mention it.

Another event—incomparably sinister—was to monopolize the entire sum of the anguish laid up in my being.

In the hall on the ground floor the gong had just sounded to announce supper. Everyone was hastening to respond to its call.

Cousin Philarète's door was the first to open and the good fellow called out to his friend Doctor Sambucus on the stairs.

"What have we got to eat this evening, Doc? I'm damnably hungry . . . You'd never imagine the appetite taxidermy gives you!"

And the old doctor replied: "You can take it from me it'll be a *gigot de canemuche*!"[24]

The steps of the Cormélon sisters resounded on the echoing tiles like those of a platoon of soldiers; as for the Dideloo family, they were already installed in the dining room before the gong had been struck.

The pulley of the plate hoist could be heard creaking and the Griboins were busily engaged with their tasks. Nancy, as befitted a proper mistress of the house, was first at her post by the table and at the serving hatch.

The call would often surprise me in some distant part of the house—sometimes in the garden when the weather was not too foul.

On this occasion I was in the drawing room, where I had just appropriated two or three candles which I intended to lay beside Lampernisse's bowl of gruel—a present I knew he would find agreeable.

I was shutting the door and making my way, without haste, to the dining room when I saw at the end of the corridor the brightly illuminated front window of the paint supplier's shop.

I found this odd: ordinarily Mathias Krook would extinguish the gas lamp and shut the shop the moment Nancy left. Then he would hurry to go and take his meal at a neighboring cookshop; and, as soon as he had put away the last mouthful, he would be back to meet my sister on the doorstep of Malpertuis, where they would chatter and laugh together until well after dark.

For some time my mind had been made up to tell the story of my adventure in the attic to somebody who would accept my singular confidences without a smile.

I had of course thought of the Abbé Doucedame, but he had not put in another appearance at Malpertuis,

Although it was only rarely that I had occasion to converse at any length with Mathias Krook, I had a good deal of fellow feeling for him.

He had a pleasant, girlish face, a brilliant, toothy smile, and showed himself distantly prepared to be friendly to me.

His attractive light tenor voice, rising from time to time from the inner recesses of the shop, made one forget the unduly brooding silences of Malpertuis. Nancy assured me that he composed his own songs—and one of them will ring like a dirge in my memory as long as I live. The seductive air, to the rhythm of a slow waltz, adapted itself (with a few hesitations) to the magnificent words of *The Song of Songs*:

I am the rose of Sharon, and the lily of the valleys . . .
Thy name is as ointment poured forth . . .[25]

Nancy was very fond of this song and, in her spells of good humor, she never tired of humming it.

As I was looking at the lighted shop, Mathias's voice arose and, in the hostile night of the house, *The Song of Songs* spoke of love and of beauty.

I had been waiting too long for the chance of a few words alone with Mathias Krook to allow the opportunity to pass.

Eagerly I traversed the corridor and entered the paint supplier's shop.

To my astonishment I found it completely empty, even though the singing came from somewhere very close by.

"*I am the rose of Sharon . . .*"

"Mathias!" I called out.

"*. . . and the lily of the valleys!*"

"Mathias Krook!" I repeated.

"*Thy name is as ointment poured forth . . .*"

The song ceased; all I now heard was the urgent murmur of the fluttering gas flame at the end of its copper pipe.

"Hey there, Mathias! Why are you hiding? There's something I want to ask you . . . No, tell you, rather . . ."

"*I am the rose of Sharon . . .*"

I leapt back, blundering against the counter.

The voice was louder. It was Mathias's voice, there was no doubting that; but it had suddenly taken on a new, and increased plangency.

"*. . . and the lily of the valleys . . .*"

I put my hands over my ears. The voice was rolling like thunder, setting the glass of the windowpanes and the jars vibrating.

"*Thy name is as ointment poured forth!*"

I could not remain there. This was no longer a human voice but a furious cataract, a tidal wave of sounds and notes breaking against the walls, shaking the vaulted ceiling, rumbling about me in a nightmarish tornado of sonorities.

I was about to flee, crying out for help, when I saw the singer.

He seemed to be standing in the angle of the door, and he seemed immense, for he stood far higher above the counter than Mathias Krook normally did.

By degrees I took in the length of his body; I could not see his head, which was lost in the shadows: but I saw his hands, long and white, his knees, which were slightly flexed and showed under the cloth of his trousers, and his feet . . .

Ah! The shimmering gaslight, as it played on his polished shoes, passed beneath them.

There was light beneath Mathias's feet!

And his feet were resting, motionless, on empty air . . . But he was singing, singing in a terrible voice that made the graduated glasses on the counter, the Roman balance with its heavy copper pans, the thousand motionless objects tremble.

It was not until I was at the far end of the hall, close to the dining room, that I found a voice to bellow out my horror.

"Mathias is dead . . . He's hanging in the shop!"

From behind the door I heard the silvery tinkle of a fork dropped to the floor, then the clamorous sound of an overturned chair; it was only after a full minute of awful silence that the voices came. Meanwhile I was frenziedly repeating:

"Hanging in the shop! Hanging in the shop!"

I was on the point of adding: "And he's still singing!" when the double doors of the dining room burst noisily open and the assembled company came rushing pell-mell into the hall.

Somebody dragged me after them. I think it was Cousin Philarète. I never saw Mathias again, for the Cormélon sisters stood shoulder to shoulder on the threshold of the shop, blocking off my view.

Over the heads of Uncle Dideloo and Aunt Sylvie I saw in the distance the bare arms of my sister, raised in the final gesture of someone drowning.

I could hear my uncle stammering: "No! no! . . . because I tell you . . . no . . ."

Then came the voice of Doctor Sambucus, piercing as the blade of a knife.

"But no . . . Krook hasn't been hanged . . . His head's been nailed to the wall!"

"His head's been nailed to the wall!" I repeated stupidly.

At this point I find myself hard put to set my memories in the right order. My mind turns to the words of Lampernisse: "Strange powers that impose on one, by turns, forgetfulness and memory." In this way it seems to me that sometimes the inhabitants of Malpertuis appear to act in full knowledge of what happens, and that for them there is no mystery, and that on other days they are no more than miserable wretches shuddering in terror before the unknown fate that lies in store. There are times when I feel that all that is required is an effort on my part in order to understand, but that a weary fatalism prevents me from gathering the resolve to do so . . .

For the moment, my mind a blank, I abandoned myself to the tide that thrust me, with the howling and gesticulating shadows, into the dining room, but before I found myself there, a fleeting vision passed before my eyes. Beside the bust of the boundary god, close by a lamp that gave off long, star-pointed rays of light, stood Lampernisse, his hands on Nancy's shoulders, and I believe I heard him murmuring: "O goddess . . . he too has been unable to hold on to the colors and the light . . ."

I cannot say how it was that Eisengott suddenly appeared among us. He stood before the inhabitants of Malpertuis like a judge at the solemn moment of pronouncing sentence.

He said: "Let's have no more of these complaints and all this idle talk!"

And then: "Nobody must know what happens in Malpertuis!

"And they cannot know!"

He interspersed these words with silences, as if he were replying to inaudible questions.

Cousin Philarète stepped forward.

"Eisengott!" he said. "I shall do what has to be done."

He went out, followed by Doctor Sambucus, whose slight stature seemed to have grown greater. Their footsteps were directed toward the paint supplier's shop, and were soon out of earshot.

"And you—all of you—take up your lives again, as Cassave intended!" Eisengott concluded.

His beard was white as driven snow and his eyes shone like gemstones.

Only Elodie spoke.

"I shall pray," she said.

Eisengott did not so much as glance at her, although the words were addressed to him.

And in fact life resumed its course, as if a thick brushstroke of tar had blotted out the events of that atrocious evening.

The very next day Nancy returned to her place in the shop; there, alone at her post, under the russet light of the gas lamp, she served the ever rarer customers. I never saw her shed a tear, nor did I hear her utter a word of complaint.

I may have been the only one who gave any further thought to that evening, vague and troubled though this thought may have been. I tried to recall how Euryale had behaved during those tragic moments and I was forced to the bewildering conclusion that she had not followed the others in their horrified stampede into the bloody shop, that she had remained motionless in her chair, her eyes fixed on her plate, in an attitude of indifference or complete mental absence.

The formidable will of Malpertuis had manifested itself to its prisoners: and they, without more ado, had bowed their heads.

So it came about that a hand the size of a fly lay severed in a corner of the attic, and that Mathias Krook, dead with his head nailed to the wall, had, in a spine-chilling voice, sung *The Song of Songs*.

4

The House on the Quai de la Balise

*Who is it then that moves about, that
keeps watch and lies in wait in this house?*
—Poritsky, *Gespenstergeschichten*[26]

I cannot claim that the peaks of terror followed each other in Malpertuis with an inexorable succession, or acquired—as in the fatal house of the Atrides—a hideous regularity like that of the tides or the phases of the moon.

Basing myself on the splendid studies of Monsieur Fresnel, I should be inclined to invoke the phenomena of interference to explain the ebb and flow that characterized the unfolding of the evil forces in Malpertuis. This produces a sort of "undulatory" phenomenon, in which the intensity of those forces varies over time.[27]

The Abbé Doucedame, who shows an increasingly marked aversion toward such subjects of conversation, was nonetheless happy enough to tell me about a kind of "fold in space," to explain the juxtaposition of two worlds, different in essence, between which Malpertuis might be considered an abominable point of contact.

However, this is merely an image and the Abbé Doucedame holds, with a somber satisfaction, that I would need an extensive knowledge of mathematics to form a clear idea of what was involved.

In this way—without remorse—he leaves me in the dark, for I never was and never will be up to much as a scholar.

There are periods of intermission in misfortune and abomination during which the Spirit of Darkness collects his thoughts, or forgets us, during which he leaves us to enjoy peace and quiet.

Cousin Philarète is becoming a good chess player and astonishes his teacher, Doctor Sambucus, who groans, with his nose glued to the board: "Philarète my lad, either you're a sly customer who's dug out a good chess manual or else you're a rascal with luck on his side."

The taxidermist stirs uneasily in his chair, sipping at a glass of milk, and Sambucus continues: "That combination of a knight and a castle following on the sacrifice of a supporting pawn . . . Ah, my boy! . . . That was a good move! You've got me there!"

Aunt Sylvie has embroidered some complicated design and Eléonore Cormélon compliments her unreservedly: "It's positively *antique* work, Madame!"

Rosalie cannot refrain from adding her contribution: "It's like a beautiful cat asleep."

"Euryale gave me the pattern," Aunt Sylvie explains.

My cousin deigns to enlighten them.

"It's the lion of the Jebel."[28]

Alice gives her a smile that is not without its particular charm.

"You draw very nicely, Mademoiselle Euryale. I see you're doing a portrait now: whose is it, I wonder?"

Euryale says, "It's the head of Princess Nefertiti."

"That's Egyptian art," I interject.

"Thank you for telling us," Euryale replies with an irony I find hurtful.

I shoot her a dark look which she disdains to notice; I am close to loving her with all my being or detesting her with all my strength. Ever since that first evening when her hand had lain on my neck and an astonishing promise had fallen from her lips, she has affected to ignore my existence.

Time and again—and each time more timidly—I propose a meeting in the garden or in the library. Sometimes she responds with a point-blank refusal; on other occasions she turns her back on me without opening her lips.

Her clothes at such times seem to me those of an old woman, her hair a trifle beyond the help of a comb, her face stony: and she is repellent . . . repellent . . .

One day I said to her: "You know, Euryale, tomorrow I shall be twenty!"

"You're almost ready to leave the cradle," was her reply.

I've promised myself to get revenge for that insult—without, however, being at all clear as to how I might do so.

And yet . . . and yet I have idea, though it is vague and confused and makes me blush and tremble.

Nancy's way of life has in no way changed. She seems to me paler, and her eyes are circled in blue shadow; she is nonetheless beautiful for that and when by chance her dress brushes against Uncle Dideloo he visibly quivers.

Outside it has stopped raining; but autumn, stripping the sky bare of clouds, has unleashed a fierce, dry east wind that presages the approach of winter.

The garden no longer has about it a hostile aspect, and I've resolved to spend a few hours there when the sun, still relatively warm, takes possession.

But the project regularly comes to naught.

I barely get as far as the edge of the pond; once there, the cold seizes me, I shiver, I draw about my throat the silk scarf without which Elodie forbids me to go out and I return to the house.

On these occasions I tell myself I will return the next day—and I do not return. Why? I have a feeling that the reason is *outside of me.*

Something—some force no doubt—considers that *what I must see there* still does not "belong" in time and I am returned to the dismal hours of the daily round.

After meals we remain a long time together in the dining room, and sometimes in the little circular drawing room, which is banal, but familiar and cheered by a splendid open fire.

The easy chairs there are spacious and deep, the carpet thick and soft. In one of the cupboards is an ample stock of liqueurs, which the men appreciate.

There we are, in the drawing room; even Nancy is with us; she has agreed to replace Uncle Dideloo in his whist game with the Cormélon sisters.

Nancy plays badly. Alice is scarcely any better and her sisters are getting annoyed.

Suddenly Rosalie bursts out: "The way you're playing! It's childish! One would never have thought you'll very soon be thirty-five, Alecta!"

Alice starts, and I see in her somber eyes a flash of fear and rage.

Perhaps she is not inclined to hear her age revealed. Perhaps . . .

Ah! It seems as if the eldest too does not take kindly to the younger one's words; she lays her hand on Rosalie's arm, who still looks pained. Why had she called her Alecta? The name is not that different from Alice, but I have the impression that that is the cause of Eléonore Cormélon's displeasure.

Sambucus also noticed it.

He has looked up; and the expression on his wrinkled face is most enigmatic.

It is beyond me ... One's life must be pretty dull for one to pay attention to such trivial things.

In my heart of hearts, and despite my grudge, I have eyes only for Euryale who, bent over her sketchbook, pencil in hand, is drawing.

But suddenly my whole being tenses: though not even granting me a look, the scheming creature has been watching me in the mirror—and the portrait she is drawing, deliberately distorted and ugly, is mine!

Sad at heart I leave the room, followed only by Alice's smile.

I wander about the deserted house where some lamps are already lit. For many days now the lamps have not been extinguished and Lampernisse no longer prowls the haunted corridors, a pitiful soul in torment; he even puts in an appearance in the kitchen, where he consents to sample Elodie's waffles and pancakes.

I return to an occupation that for some little time has provided me with a wholly innocent pleasure: I spy on the Griboins! It is a poor pastime, and one that affords few discoveries.

By way of a little leaded window whose curtain is only half drawn, I am able to observe them without being seen. Their concierge's lodge, which serves also as a kitchen, is very cramped and the gloomiest room in the house. A pallid light seeps in from a transom window, casting grotesque shadows from the least of objects. When their services are not required about the house, the Griboins sit at a deal table covered with a red plush cloth.

Wearing a droopy, tasseled nightcap, Griboin smokes a long, brown pipe; his wife, her hands laid flat on her knees, is lost in reverie, her eyes fixed unseeing on the figures in the large *image d'Épinal*[29] on the wall facing her. Only very rarely do they speak a word to one another.

To tell the truth there is really nothing worth seeing in that double immobility; and yet I spend a considerable time at that curtained window, watching them, and I try to understand what goes on in the minds of those two creatures, happy in their inertia and their silence.

All the same, there are moments when the Griboins shake off the leaden weight that bears down upon them.

The wife would vanish into a corner where she would be lost in the shadows; when she reappeared she would be carrying a brown leather bag; then Griboin would lay down his pipe and pass a pointed tongue over his black lips. They were going to count their money.

They count! and count!

Their faces change; now they are a pair of huge, sharp-clawed rats piling up heaps of *écus* and *jaunets*.[30]

Their parched lips move, and in their movement I read the mounting total, interspersed with an inaudible watchword: "We must save up . . . we must save up . . ."

The gold and silver coins do not chink, and when the Griboin woman rakes them together with a spidery gesture to return them to the leather purse they make no sound.

The woman disappears again into the darkness; then she resumes her place at the table, her hands on her knees, and Griboin relights his pipe with a smoky lump of charcoal from the stove, whose filthy stench seems to reach me through the glass of my observation post.

Then I get the idea of giving them a fright. Without knowing why, I suddenly cried out: "Tchiek! . . ."

An earthquake would not have been more disturbing to the old people, intoxicated with money and solitude.

To make myself understood I must go back a little in my account.

At Malpertuis there are never any visitors other than those I have mentioned, with the exception of a creature so ludicrous that the majority of the inhabitants are still unaware of him.

Once a week the Griboin woman sets about a thorough cleaning of the enormous house and, thanks to the aid of their helper, everything there shines and glitters within a matter of hours.

Dressed in a coarse homespun coat, wearing a sort of tricorn hat that seems screwed down on his enormous round head, this drudge has the appearance of a hogshead mounted on thick legs with feet like cooking pots; arms of a simian length complete this rough sketch of the human form. He lifts huge wooden buckets, filled with water, and plies fantastic brooms and floor cloths the size of coverlets with an indescribable vigor.

The heaviest objects seem to slide along or rise up of themselves at his approach; despite his bulk he moves and works at an extraordinary pace. When he cuts the stacks of firewood into little logs, his axe dances in the air and the chips whiz about him like hailstones in a hailstorm.

I had taken care not to question the Griboins concerning him: *one does not ask such questions in Malpertuis*—that is the rule one adheres to there, immediately and of one's own accord.

One day I resolved to see his face, and my resolve cost me a shock of utter disgust: he had no face.

In the shadow of the tricorn there was only a broad expanse of pink and gleaming flesh, with three small openings at the places of the eyes and the mouth.

The Griboin woman directed his operations by gestures and never spoke a word to him; he, for his part, emitted at rare intervals a single, brief sound, like the beak-clacking of a twilight nightjar.

"Tchiek! Tchiek!"

Where did he come from? Where did he go, his duty done?

Once—only once—I saw the Griboin woman lead him into the garden and vanish with him under the trees.

One day, then, when the couple, having satisfied their miserly joys, had resumed their dejected attitude, I uttered the cry "Tchiek! Tchiek!" And, believe me, I imitated it very well.

Griboin dropped his pipe and his wife threw her arms in the air, letting out a wild, hooting cry.

They rushed to the door together, shooting the bolts and shoving the table and chairs against it as a barricade.

From somewhere in the obscurity of the lodge Griboin unearthed a cutlass and I heard him screaming angrily: "You!... it's you!... Who else but you!"

"Impossible, I tell you! Completely im-poss-ible!" she wailed, her face drawn and haggard.

I thought it best not to repeat this most successful prank, fearing I know not what discovery; but I knew that Malpertuis concealed yet another mystery.

One morning in the week of my twentieth birthday I went down into the kitchen at the hour when Elodie was stoking up her stoves for the midday meal. Doctor Sambucus was keeping her company, drinking a little glass of Spanish wine and nibbling biscuits.

"Elodie," I said, "give me the key to our house."

"The key to our house?" our servant asked, astonished.

"But yes ... Our house on the Quai de la Balise. I want to go there after dinner."

It was the first time since our coming to Malpertuis that I had made up my mind to escape from it for a few hours.

Elodie hesitated. In her honest look I read fear and reprobation.

Sambucus was singing quietly to himself: "*When the young bird sprouts its wings . . .*"

Elodie blushed and said very quietly: "You ought to be ashamed!"

"But no!" the Doctor protested. "On the contrary! If the emperor of Cathay lived amid the admiration, the respect, and love of his subjects, it was because at the age of ten he already maintained seven hundred wives!"

"I held him in my arms when he was *so* little . . . and to think . . ."

Elodie turned aside, and I heard her choke on a sob.

"Give him the key, all the same, Elodie."

With a heavy sigh she went and fumbled in the drawer of a deep dresser. Without another word she handed me the key I had asked for.

With a strange and delicious anguish in my heart, I slipped away; in the darkness of the staircase I heard the rustling of a dress: but I saw no one.

At dinner I scarcely touched the dishes set before me, and I was mocked by Cousin Philarète who did full justice to hearty, grilled steaks and no less lavish helpings of fowl.

I kept a covert watch on the others, as if my least gesture would betray my plan of a magnificent escape.

As always, they were indifferent to anything that did not garnish their plates.

Uncle continued to sneak glances at Nancy, whose thoughts were elsewhere; Sambucus was drawing Philarète's attention to the finer points of the menu; the Cormélon sisters, with the exception of the inwardly smiling Alice, were eating as if they were in a rush;

Aunt Sylvie was mopping her plate with an enormous hunk of bread; Euryale was absorbed in staring at the glittering reflections in her glass; the Griboins were gliding about from one to the other like puppets mounted on castors.

When the moment came to cross the threshold into the street, the fear seized me that some mysterious event might intervene that would prevent me from putting my plan into action.

I glanced fearfully about me, but nothing moved in the eternal darkness of the place; only, in the distance, the boundary god stared at me with his eyes of white stone.

The street received me with a broad smile; in a sidelong ray of sunshine sparrows were bickering over a wisp of straw; in the distance a fishmonger's rattle was whirring.

All at once faces loomed out of the golden afternoon; they belonged to ordinary people attending to ordinary tasks. They did not so much as glance at me, but I would happily have planted kisses on all those unknown cheeks.

On a humpbacked bridge whose narrow span vaulted the green waters of the river, an old man was dangling his line in the stream.

"It may be cold, but I've caught a couple of bream," he called out as I passed.

Outside the window of a baker's shop a flour-covered pastry cook's apprentice poured out a basketful of steaming, newly baked rolls and, in the window of a tavern, a couple of pipe smokers gravely clinked their blue stoneware pots, brimming with fresh foam.

All these simple images breathed forth life in abundance; I inhaled the chilly air of the street that seemed perfumed with the hot rolls and the frothy beer and enlivened by the song of the river and the delight of the old bream fisher.

At the corner of the Quai de la Balise our old house came in sight, its green shutters closed.

The key was a little difficult to turn in the lock, and the door creaked on its hinges as it opened. This was all the blame that that sweet and quiet dwelling laid against me for a long abandonment.

I saluted Nicolas Grandsire, tall and severe in his faded gold frame, and hastened to the drawing room, witness to so many tranquil hours.

A vague odor of fustiness and vetiver hung in the air, but the logs in the hearth were ready for kindling.

At the first flame the house awoke and was welcoming. The broad divan, on which Nancy had heaped up an improbable quantity of cushions, invited me to rest; books, forsaken but for all that never forgotten, lit up the prism of their multicolored bindings behind the glass doors of the bookcase.

Knickknacks flirtatiously sought to make me forget that a little dust had dimmed their beauty; pink conch shells began once more to imitate the sound of the sea at my approach. Countless small tokens of affections melted into one to welcome me and keep me among them.

In a corner of the mantelpiece I came upon the Abbé Doucedame's cherry-wood pipe and his glazed earthenware tobacco jar.

I was apprehensive of the harsh joys of the fragrant weed, but a fond recollection of my excellent teacher caused me to fill the pipe and light it.

I am still amazed at the triumphal entry I made into the paradise of smokers: my being experienced no revulsion and, from the first puffs, my delight was absolute.

It was the triple pleasure of my temporarily regained liberty, of my rediscovered surroundings and my solitary initiation into tobacco that caused me to forget that I was expecting...

I was expecting I knew not what; but I had left Malpertuis in the certainty of that expectation.

And I spoke that certainty aloud.

"I'm expecting... I'm expecting..."

I took as witness the objects surrounding me, I asked the knickknacks dressed in light dust, the roar of the conch shells, the delicate curls of blue smoke for an answer.

"I'm expecting... I'm expecting..."

Suddenly the response came: a high-pitched bell sounded timidly in the hallway.

My heart contracted and, for some moments, fear held me captive on the divan amid the warm delight of the cushions.

The bell renewed its call more insistently.

I had the impression that a very long interval elapsed between the moment of my rising from the divan and the moment when, passing the portrait of Nicolas Grandsire in the hall, I opened the door.

A veiled silhouette stood there in the golden mildness of the afternoon; she entered without a sound, slipped like a shadow through the hall to the drawing room and the divan.

The veils fell: I recognized a smile; strong hands grasped me by the shoulders, drawing me down, while burning lips took possession of mine.

Alice Cormélon had come ... I knew now that it was her I was expecting, *that it could only have been her.*

The flaming logs exhaled a torrid scent of burning resin; the tobacco smoke had a fragrance of spices and honey, and from Alice's veils and her clothes, as they fell with a muffled sound to the deeply carpeted floor, there arose the heady redolence of rose and amber.

>⤛

Twilight was insinuating itself over the slopes of the darkening roofs, the fire crumbling into cinders and the mirrors becoming swamped with black waters when Alice knotted up her long, ebony-and-jet hair.

"Time to go," she murmured in a whisper.

"We'll stay here," I said, crushing her to me fiercely.

Without any effort she disengaged herself from my feeble embraces; beneath the marvelous ivory tint of her arms she was in full control of her powerful muscles.

"Shall we come back then?"

It was already too dark for me to read anything in her eyes.

"Perhaps," she sighed.

Her dress rose about the forms that had uncovered their adorable mystery and the veils were back in place.

Suddenly she grasped me in her arms, shuddering with terror.

"Listen ... there's somebody walking about in the house!"

I listened and shuddered in turn: a slow and heavy tread was advancing, leaving a hollow vacancy in the silence.

I could not have said whether it was descending from the floor above or coming up from the cellars: its sound filled the void, and yet it awoke no sonority or resonance.

It advanced across the hall and halted abruptly at the door of the drawing room where Alice and myself stood motionless, frozen in terror.

At any moment I expected to see that door turn slowly on its hinges and open onto the mystery of that sound.

It did not open.

But, in the evening gloom a voice spoke, slow and doleful:

"Alecta! Alecta! Alecta!"

Three separate blows were struck on the door and three times my heart leapt in my breast, as if those blows had been struck at the depths of my being.

Alice reeled on her feet, stiffened, and precipitately opened the door.

The hall was empty; the green light from the window flooded it like a forgotten reflection of the moon.

"Come," she said.

We found ourselves in the street at the gentle hour when the lamps are lit.

"Alecta . . ." I said.

She let out a fierce cry and seized my shoulder in a bone-cracking grip.

"Never . . . you understand? . . . never . . . never speak that name—unless you wish misfortune and terror to come upon you!"

At the corner, by the bridge, she left me without a word of farewell, and I have no idea what route she took to return to Malpertuis, for she was there on my return and I had not dallied on the way.

Elodie took the key from me without asking any questions.

I sat down by the fire where the braised steaks were gently dribbling in the casseroles.

"Elodie! I've brought back the Abbé Doucedame's pipe and his jar of tobacco. I think I'm going to enjoy smoking very much."

Doctor Sambucus, who had just come in and who had heard, backed me up.

"It does me good to hear that, my lad. Knowing you smoke a pipe, it seems to me there's another man under the roof of Malpertuis, and God knows we have few enough!"

Elodie uttered not a word; it was plain she was in a bad mood.

I left the kitchen, followed by Sambucus.

On the landing the doctor took my arm.

"Listen!" he said.

In the distance there arose the sound of lamentation.

"It's Lampernisse; he's started again. The lamps are going out again!"

And away he went with his quick-tripping, birdlike walk.

In the hallway I ran into Nancy. She drew me into the corner where the boundary god held sway and regarded me earnestly in the light of the clay lamp that burned there.

"Oh, Jiji! What's going on? . . . What's happened to you? You're completely different . . . and it's only a few hours ago that you left me. You . . . you're suddenly like your father's portrait . . ."

She set her lips against my hair but immediately backed away with a cry of grief.

"You smell of rose and amber . . . Oh, my Jiji!"

She fled into the darkness and I heard her weeping bitterly.

I was standing there motionless, leaning against the stone god's pedestal, when a voice of a heartrending sadness arose in the darkness:

"The goddess is weeping ... They have stolen the light from her eyes and her heart!"

The evening came to a close in the round drawing room: chess, whist, and embroidery—embroidery, whist, and chess.

Alice played well and was complimented; she blushed with pleasure.

Euryale rose, let fall the pencil she had been toying with, and took a turn about the great table.

When she arrived behind Alice she halted and appeared interested in her hand of cards; I saw at once, though, that it was not upon the variegated pieces of cardboard that Euryale's gaze was fastened but on Alice's neck, that white, rather long, infinitely gracious neck, from which I had with such difficulty detached my lips.

Euryale's body was vibrating with a cruel vitality; her hands rose, reaching to the level of that neck.

Alice was still smiling, her thoughts elsewhere, unaware of my cousin's mute rage.

I felt no fear: a sense of pride triumph blazed out in my heart.

"She's jealous! Euryale is jealous!"

I did not ask myself if she was aware of my amorous escapade. I could only rejoice inwardly.

"She's jealous!"

For a brief moment I could've wished to see her ferocious talons clamped about the young woman's throat, but nothing so final occurred; Euryale's hands dropped and were lost in the folds of her black dress; she continued her round of the table and insinuated herself behind me.

I kept my eyes fixed on the pier glass facing me; for lack of illumination it was completely dark.

Suddenly two dreadful points of light pierced its gloom and I saw again, for the second time, the terrible tiger eyes that fixed me; but this time, instead of streaming opalescent gleams they were burning with an indescribable fury.

I did not turn my head.

5

Exit Dideloo ... Exit Nancy ... Exit Tchiek

> *There are crimes which God alone can avenge.*
>
> —The Book of Enoch[31]

For the third time now, on the staircase, I had slipped a note into Alice's hand in which I had asked for a second rendezvous in the house on the Quai de la Balise.

Hide your reply under the bust of the boundary god, I had begged by way of conclusion.

The boundary god and Cupid, prince of love affairs, have nothing in common; at the third pressing and miserable appeal a square of paper bears a brief—indeed monosyllabic—reply: *No!*

All my cunning moves to bring about an encounter with the youngest of the Cormélon sisters have come to nothing.

I lie in wait for Alice as for a prey; and she escapes my ambushes with an adroitness that is tinged with malice, until such time as chance enlightens me as to the reason for her refusal and succeeds in breaking my heart.

It was one of those featureless days when nothing occurs to trouble the strange sleep of Malpertuis, when all the mystery and terror that that house encompasses is absent, or subject to the mysterious law of intermission.

In the yellow drawing room—which we rarely enter, so hostile is it to our presence—Uncle Dideloo was writing furiously.

The door was half ajar and I saw him bent over his work, his brow moist, his eyes fevered.

At length, with a nervous gesture, he blotted the sheet he had written, sealed it in an envelope and hurriedly left the room.

I slipped in after him and took possession of the blotting paper.

Uncle Dideloo's writing was large and clear; and it was traced with a broad-cut quill pen, so that the blotting paper reproduced it faithfully, in reverse.

It was a small step to hold up the sheet to the revelation of a mirror. Ah, my heart, my poor, twenty-year-old heart . . .

My beloved Alice,

I must see you again. But our meetings here in Malpertuis itself are becoming more and more risky. Try as I might to convince myself that nobody sees us, I feel that attentive—and dangerous—eyes are fixed upon us from the deepest shadows. We must escape for a few hours from this house of peril. I have been looking for a roof to give an obliging shelter to our moments of tenderness and, at last, I have found one!

Hold on to this address: 7, Rue de la Tête Perdue.

It is an alleyway, which most people do not know is there, starting from the far side of the Place des Ormes and running into the Pré-aux-Oies.

At number 7 lives la mère *Groulle, an old woman, half deaf and blind, who is very fond of money but is not so deaf as to fail to hear the three rings at the bell which will induce her to open the door, even late at night. She will open the door to you then, even if you ring at*

*midnight, and will not recognize you, nor even look at you. You climb
the stairs before you: two doors open off the landing.*

The room, our room, *is the one that looks out over the little garden. It cannot but please you: in the days of her one-time glory* la mère
Groulle *must have been a person of taste.*

*I shall be waiting for you this evening at midnight. It is not very
difficult to leave Malpertuis, where everybody is in bed by ten (provided they don't insist on a game of whist).*

*This is a request . . . Don't oblige me, my beloved Alice, to turn it
into a command. In that case I shall call you Alecta . . .*

    Your own,
      Charles

I let fall the blotting paper, the betrayer of such crime, and ran
to the garden to hide my tears of rage and shame.

It was only when the last of these were drying in the harsh
northerly wind that was shaking the trees that I recalled the last
sentence of the letter—and its threat: *In that case I shall call you
Alecta!*

Why did that name—so close to the name Alice—fill the fearful eyes of Eléonore Cormélon with wrath?

What mysterious voice had pronounced that name in the twilight of our house on the Quai de la Balise, and why had Alice cried
out in fear—to such a degree as to threaten me?

The heart's sorrows are not exempt from a certain bitter
pleasure; I understood this when I returned to the yellow drawing
room to retrieve the blotting paper and reread the words that had
so wounded me.

It was no longer there.

I did not give the matter much thought, assuming that Uncle Dideloo, realizing his lack of prudence, had recovered it.

I saw Alice again at dinner: a slight flush about her cheeks, an excited light in her eyes told me the letter had reached its destination; Uncle Dideloo's cock-a-hoop manner left me in no doubt as to the response . . .

Alice had accepted the midnight assignation!

Perhaps everything would have come to an end for me in an outburst of tears, some resentment, and then healthy forgetfulness had not Dideloo, intoxicated with his victory, poked fun at my youth.

Doctor Sambucus, in the mood for philosophical discussion, launched into a discourse on the eternal verities, invoking Cicero's *De Senectute*.[32]

Dideloo registered his agreement and went one better.

"To think," he remonstrated, "that teachers put a work such as that into the hands of snotty-nosed whippersnappers like our friend Jean-Jacques. Ah, that's what you might call casting pearls before swine!"

I blushed with fury, which seemed to please him mightily.

"Don't fret yourself, little lad," he concluded in a mawkish and patronizing tone, "you still have your humming tops and glass marbles."

I gritted my teeth and brusquely left the dining room from which I heard a burst of laughter.

"Scum!" I grumbled sullenly. "We'll see soon enough what sort of a face you'll pull when . . ."

Once again my plan was vague and ill defined; and it did not become any clearer until suppertime when, once again, I saw Alice.

Jealousy wracked my inmost being; rancor inflamed me like a traitorous wine.

That was what clinched the matter . . .

~~~

An officer of the night watch, bearing a halberd, was crying half-past eleven at the corner of Rue du Vieux Chantier as I silently shut the door behind me.

Uncle Dideloo had rightly predicted bedtime in Malpertuis: from ten o'clock onward everything there became quiet and somber, lightless apart from the eternal lamps that bestarred the corridors, and which no spirit of darkness came to menace.

Some festival or other was still enlivening the town for, behind the red-lit windows of the taverns, songs and bursts of laughter could be heard and from time to time I encountered drunken revelers speaking their thoughts aloud to the moon.

Here and there, at the remote corners of deserted streets, the dying lights of a few Chinese lanterns still glimmered.

To reach the Place des Ormes I had to cross a street of doubtful reputation, lined with disreputable drinking houses. On the threshold of one of these a group of masked feasters importuned me: "Hey you, handsome boy, come and stand us a drink!"

I continued on my way without looking back, pursued by gibes and coarse jests.

The street petered out in darkness, the pavement skirting a row of forbidding houses lit by a hanging lantern.

In its light was a night owl, standing quite motionless, his eyes raised to the sky. He was draped in a black, hooded cloak and as I drew closer I saw that he too was a participant in the expiring festivities, for a mask covered his face.

But what a mask . . .

I remember that, when I was a child, Elodie had cut out of one of my picture books a print of the Devil painting masks. The Evil One was bent over a cardboard visage, which he was transforming, with rapid brushstrokes, into a nameless horror.

A brief glimpse of that image had thrown me into convulsions, and Elodie had removed it once and for all from my horrified attention.

Now the mask raised to the stars evoked that print so vividly that I leapt to one side.

The solitary figure made no move; he did not seem to notice my presence or my terror. He remained pressed against the wall, with his head raised, and the light of the lantern falling on the appalling grimace of his mask.

I passed him hurriedly.

I turned when I reached the corner; he had vanished. I found myself on the Place des Ormes. Here the houses were further apart, leaving space for a few trees and broadening out an expanse of sky in which a crescent moon was rising.

A shadow momentarily effaced the sickle moon as it passed across it; and yet not a cloud troubled the purity of that icy sky.

The shadow passed over the trees, then over the houses; in front of me something fell to earth with a soft, muffled sound; I saw a small, dead owl, its silvery belly stained with blood.

I rang three times at number seven on the Rue de la Tête Perdue; an old woman opened the door, clenched her hand over the coins I held out to her, and immediately turned her back on me.

A staircase, lit by a Venetian glass lamp, led in narrow flights to the upper story.

Somewhere on the ground floor the old woman began talking out loud, confiding her strange utterances to a cat.

Leaning over the banister rail I could see her huddled in an enormous plush armchair, the cat, which she called Lupka, in her lap.

I realized that for years now she had been all but blind, and that she lived in a permanent semi-sleep that rendered actual, complete sleep useless to her.

When the bell rang she knew, from the shudder that ran along Lupka's back, that she must receive visitors and their money.

Ah yes, they were strange things that she intoned!

"The gods are getting a new taste for life, Lupka; but it is the detestable life of men that falls to their lot. It's splendid though, splendid, and it gladdens me. Listen! You don't like me saying it . . . nor Him either, eh? I don't care . . . for that's the wretched part I had to play!

"Three times the velvety water has flowed over your skin, Lupka," she sang softly; "I opened the door and he put a gold coin in my hand. Gold is warm and it warms my heart through my callused flesh; silver is colder and its sweetness does not mount so high in my veins. What sort of a man is it that my eyes refuse to see? Tell me then, Lupka, whose shudders are a language. Well, well, I know now . . . a slug sticking to the wheel of fortune, over which the divine foot is poised.

"I accepted the warm gold as one accepts love . . . and the hand that brushed against mine was not quite that of a man. Not that I care . . . Who is it, though, that would oppose the workings of fate? Who is he? Where is he? What is he doing? What does it matter to me, that's what I say; but since the breath that animates the marvelous forest of your fur is so very talkative tonight, I cannot but listen. A flame fluttering in the wind of pain and fear? What are you saying? In the other room, attentive to everything that's happening and will happen in the next room? Ah, Lupka, there was a time when that meant nothing else but 'youth'!

"Be quiet . . . be quiet! I forbid you to look, Lupka!

"*That* one hasn't rung three times on the bell of love—no need for that. She hasn't given me gold, for I wasn't obliged to open the door to her. Be quiet, be quiet . . . your whole being is crackling with sparks, and you, who are a demon, you render a terrified homage . . .

"Aha! three rings of the bell, I must open the door.

"The rest belongs to the night."

And thus, on the borderlands of dream, *la mère* Groulle soliloquized.

⚬━◄

Sounds rose up the stairwell. I left my observation post, feeling no more interest in those empty words and repressing the nausea that rose to my lips at such a downfall.

I reached the room looking out over the little garden.

The door was open and it was still empty.

My heart contracted as I admitted to myself that that black-guard Dideloo had neither lied nor exaggerated when he had promised Alice a worthy love nest.

I still wonder how it came about that that mean and dingy house, where the air stagnated, heavy with the stale odor of fustiness, could, under its moss-grown roof, shelter such a marvel of warm tenderness.

Veiled in shades of transparent silk, candles were burning, set in mother-of-pearl candlesticks; a fire of small, crackling logs was dancing in the depths of a fireplace of the finest marble.

It took some time to make out the precise forms of the furniture: everything there was white, mauve, and soft in outline, as if at the heart of a huge snowball.

An obstinate scent of tuberose floated in the mild air and, on a silver bracket, an hourglass counted the moments by the crystalline fall of its tears.

I stood there a while bewitched before it came to me that in those dreamlike surroundings my first love was dying away; but the bitter sentiment of jealousy was soon replaced by another: a nameless terror reigned in that atmosphere of abandon. I felt nonetheless that I remained a stranger to that incommensurable anguish, that it was outside of me, that, whilst brushing against me, it was pursuing some other end.

I was seized by a violent desire to warn Alice and Uncle Dideloo of the peril I foresaw, but a will opposed to my own was already usurping my actions.

I backed out of the room and, like a sleepwalker, found my way to the other. Footsteps were approaching up the staircase.

Ugh! A cesspool replaced the white and mauve Eden; through the curtainless windows an insolent moonlight shamelessly illuminated the sordidness of the place.

The door of my retreat was open and the Venetian glass lamp lit up the landing; the silhouette of Uncle Dideloo was thrown on the dimly lit, color-streaked wall.

He seemed to me ugly and ridiculous in his great puce hooded overcoat and his rigid little felt hat.

As he came up the stairs he was whistling one of the vulgar tunes that had pursued me through the festive streets.

I heard him grunting with pleasure when he entered the marvelous room and the next moment, to my fury, he began in his tremulous voice to sing poor Mathias Krook's *Song of Songs*:

"*I am the rose of Sharon . . .*

"*Thy name is as ointment poured forth . . .*"

Ah, the wretch! To that song, so moving, sanctified by the blood of Matthias, he had added his own words—words so dissolute as to turn my stomach:

"*. . . perfume disperses, disperses,*

"*Tiddly-tursus, tiddly-tarsus,*

"*Thirty-six legs make eighteen . . .*"

Only the magnitude of the horror prevented me from running to him, flinging my contempt in his face, and boxing his ears. For the horror came . . .

An enormous, black form silently mounted the stairs, stepped over the banister rail, slipped toward the room where Dideloo was still bellowing.

I recognized the frightful masked figure from the street.

It passed my door and was bathed in the moonlight.

I saw that what I had taken for a repellent cardboard mask was an unbelievable reality.

The hood had fallen back and laid bare the head of the intruder in all its frightfulness. It was huge, chalky white, and pierced with bloodshot, flaming eyeballs. The mouth was immense and black, the lips drawn back in a mirthless grin over a catlike set of teeth, with overgrown canines, licked by a narrow, cleft tongue.

A black vapor undulated in a monstrous aureole about that hellish muzzle; I saw it rising and falling like boiling pitch and then, suddenly, punctured with innumerable eyes, cruel and fixed: serpents, lacquered in darkness, were twisting and thrashing about that demoniacal skull.

For a few seconds the monstrosity remained still, as if to give me time to look my fill on its boundless hideousness; then it threw back its cloak and revealed membranous wings and claws of gleaming steal.

With a howl that set the whole decrepit building shaking it hurled itself into the room where Dideloo was singing.

I in my turn let out a cry of terror and I tried to rush out of the room; I even think that, despite my unutterable fear, I would have sought to go to Uncle Dideloo's aid.

Something held me back.

Something was pressing down on my arm, heavy as lead.

A hand, very large and very beautiful, as if carved in old ivory.

It materialized out of the darkness and I saw only it.

Slowly it drew me to the window and I saw the sky. It was in the grip of an unbelievable tumult; I saw gigantic wings gliding in the moonlight, eyes lit with a violent red fury, monstrous claws grasping at haunted space. In the midst of those forms tormented by an infernal rage, ninety feet from the ground, a human form was struggling and I recognized Uncle Dideloo.

I cried out; but a roll of thunder and flashes of lightning drowned that feeble cry of distress.

The ivory hand was no longer weighing down on my arm; I saw it still, though, vanishing into the distance like a white flame.

But now a silhouette appeared, still very vague in the darkness of the room.

A long frockcoat . . . a silvery beard, eyes that were severe and at the same time infinitely sad.

"Eisengott!"

There was no longer anyone there to reply: the phantom had vanished. Sobbing, I rushed out of the detestable hovel.

The storm had ceased abruptly. The sky was pure, given over to the diamond-strewn splendor of the stars and the soft light of the moon.

I ran to the Place des Ormes and, in the distance, I saw stretched out the body of Uncle Dideloo.

But I did not approach it: a thickset figure emerged from the shadow of the trees.

I recognized Cousin Philarète.

He walked over to the corpse, lifted it without emotion, and carried it off into the night.

And nobody ever spoke of Uncle Dideloo again—NOT ONCE!

Under the dominion of what mysterious force do we live, no longer to concern ourselves with him, as if he had never been one of us, as if he had never existed?

Henceforth at meals Aunt Sylvie sat next to Rosalie Cormélon, onetime table companion of my uncle, and it seemed to be the most natural thing in the world for her.

As soon as we found ourselves alone in the kitchen, I mentioned the name of the departed to Elodie.

She was staring into the fire; without raising her eyes, she said, "We must pray! In this life we must always pray."

It was toward Christmas that my sister Nancy left us.

She did so in the most straightforward of ways.

One morning, as we were drinking coffee in the kitchen—Elodie, Doctor Sambucus and myself—she came in, dressed in an ample broadcloth coat and carrying a traveling bag.

"I'm leaving you," she said. "I'm giving up all the assets that were promised to me. God willing, I shall keep watch over Jiji from afar."

"God go with you," Elodie murmured, without evincing the least surprise.

"Adieu, my beauty," said Sambucus, biting, without further ado, into a thin slice of buttered bread.

I caught up with her on the stairs and took hold of the hem of her coat; but she pushed me away gently.

"My destiny is not to remain in Malpertuis. And I'm sure it isn't yours, Jiji," she said gravely.

"You'll be going back to our house on the Quai de la Balise, Nancy?"

She shook her splendid, somber head.

"Oh no! . . . no!"

She left without a backward glance, and the street door fell to behind her with a final, thunderous crash.

I made my way to the paint supplier's. It was empty.

Carboys, glass jars, balances, packing cases and bottles—all were gone.

In a corner I heard a sound like the nibbling of mice, and there I found Lampernisse, finishing off his bowl of gruel.

I told him of Nancy's departure; but he seemed not to hear me and appeared to be taking a certain pleasure in his wretched repast.

And then, amid the seasonal ice and snow, Christmas came.

>⟁~

Before coming to that memorable night, which brought peace and hope to others but swamped Malpertuis in unclean terror, I must here report a double interlude which could not but increase my disquiet and my fear. More and more frequently I was in the habit of wandering about the house where everybody avoided one another outside of those ineluctable hours of mealtime community. On two or three occasions those haphazard wanderings led me to the upper floor, very close to the trapdoor to the attics.

I did not raise it: silence reigned beyond that closed barrier, although from time to time it seemed to me I heard very light steps which *could* have been the alarmed flight of mice or the furtive awakening of bats, snatched for a few instants from their winter somnolence. Seated at the foot of the stairs, hoping for something that might divert my thoughts from the distress and abandonment that endlessly obscured my life, I would take out of my pocket the

Abbé Doucedame's pipe and seek forgetfulness in the philosophical delights of tobacco.

During one of these moments of relative euphoria, a door was stealthily opened and I heard a murmur of voices.

"Well now, Sambucus, am I right or not?"

It was Cousin Philarète, speaking in a tone that struck me as being deeply worried.

"Well! yes, it would appear so," the doctor replied. "That's the smell of his wretched Dutch tobacco. He's the only one that smokes it!"

"I tell you the Abbé's prowling about the place. We've got to watch out for that holy crow!"

"It's been weeks since he was last here!" the old physician grumbled.

"I tell you, Sambucus, we've got to watch out for him. Once a Doucedame, always a Doucedame, even if he's got up as a priest!"

"Take it easy, my friend. After all, it's not so very long now till Candlemas night."

"Shhh! You're letting your tongue run away with you, Doc, what with the house full of the smell of his detestable tobacco."

"I'm telling you . . ."

"Say nothing!"

The door was slammed violently. A muffled rumor mounted from below, interspersed with furious repetitions of "Tchiek! Tchiek!"

It was cleaning day and the Griboin woman must have been piloting the misshapen domestic about the corridors.

The enormous footsteps of the powerful mass of flesh mounted toward me, then suddenly stopped.

I leaned over the banister rail to catch sight of the Griboin woman briskly turning and going back down the stairs, four at a time, abandoning her assistant.

Tchiek stood motionless, like an automaton whose works have unexpectedly broken down, arms dangling, legs apart.

I left my vantage point and went close to him, to touch him.

"Tchiek!" I murmured. "Tchiek!"

He didn't move. I touched his hand. It was cold and hard as stone.

"Tchiek!"

I brushed my hand against his brow.

I pulled it away in disgust. Once again I had touched cold stone; but this time it was viscous, as if it had just been picked out of the sewer.

"Psst! Look out, my child!"

Startled, I looked up: two feet above my head Lampernisse was hanging over the banisters.

"Look out, my child! The Griboin woman's coming back!"

"What is that?" I asked in a low voice, pointing at the repugnant statue of flesh.

He began laughing.

"It's nothing!"

"But what?"

Lampernisse laughed even harder.

"Later on, when the time comes and the Griboin woman is done with him, just go down to the garden. You know where the little wooden shed is, the one where Griboin keeps his fishing tackle? Yes? Well, lift up his nets. But I tell you, it's nothing . . . nothing . . ."

And when I remained standing there before him, irresolute and dissatisfied, he resumed that mysterious air of confidence I had seen about him one day on the stairs leading to the attics.

"Nothing . . . there was a time though when he was something great, something enormous. That brute used to lift mountains as easily as he shifts the Griboin woman's buckets these days. Drunk with power and pride, he led the most terrible rebellion! Tchiek! . . . Tchiek! . . . That's the sound made by the bodies of the vanquished, falling into the abyss . . . Tchiek! . . . Tchiek! . . . barely the cry of a dying bird!"

All at once he stopped laughing and fled; the Griboin woman was returning.

I retreated into the darkness and, a moment later, I heard again the misshapen creature's cries of "Tchiek! Tchiek!"

In the afternoon I followed Lampernisse's advice.

The shed was close to the high wall that surrounded the vast garden of Malpertuis. The door, which lacked latch or lock, hung half open.

Old Griboin's fishing tackle was stacked neatly in the corner, next to some garden tools and a disused wheelbarrow. Coarse brown fishing nets were piled high in another corner.

I lifted them and my hands trembled when I touched a large, hard felt hat.

Tchiek was there, curled up on himself, cold and inert.

"I told you: nothing!"

I turned and saw Lampernisse, brandishing a stout, rusty harpoon.

"Nothing! . . . nothing! . . . Just you see!"

Before I could stay his hand the harpoon had struck home, full in the stony face.

I cried out in terror when I heard a serpent-like hiss and saw Tchiek fall in upon himself and disappear.

"You see!" Lampernisse exulted.

Among the nets of coarse, brown cord there was now only a rumpled skin and a sticky suit of rough, homespun cloth.

"Lampernisse!" I implored, "tell me what's just happened!"

"I've shown that he was … nothing," Lampernisse roared, shaking with laughter; but then, all at once, he was again sullen and distant.

"A slave; and it's only right … Bah! Philarète, that miserable flunky of Cassave's, will attend to him, if he's still worth the trouble," he grumbled as he left me.

I returned to the house. As I walked up the steps to the door I felt an icy caress on my cheek; the first snowflakes were hovering in the twilight.

6

The Christmas Nightmare

Who is this that darkens counsel by words without knowledge?

—Zechariah[33]

What would the gods be, were it not for terror?

—(Imitation of the Scriptures)

Christmas Eve came, stripped of all the joyful anticipation of the great feast to follow. In the morning I had found the kitchen dark and cold, its fires unlit. Elodie made no response to my calls, and I sensed that she too had left us; but she had left without a word of farewell, without a backward glance at everything she had loved.

At midday the Griboins served a detestable meal, which nobody touched. Something indefinable was floating in the air: fear, the agony of expectation, the premonition of disaster—how am I to say?

Curled up in his chair, Doctor Sambucus was like a skinny and snappish weasel holding itself ready for a final bite. Cousin Philarète was staring at me with his heavy, sea-green eyes; but he did not see me, of that I was certain.

The Cormélon sisters were in the shadows, motionless; since they were sitting with their backs to the light, I could not see their faces.

Aunt Sylvie, her back pressed firmly against the back of her chair, was asleep, her mouth open, her teeth gleaming.

Euryale...

Her chair was empty; yet I could've sworn that, the moment before, she had been in her customary place, wearing her dismal, nunnish dress, her eyes staring into space or obstinately fixed on a design in the tablecloth or on her plate.

I turned and saw the Griboins busy at the dessert tables, their faces repulsively pale; possibly the reason for this pallor lay in the reflection from the snow.

This snow which for days had been piling up in all its white patience was now falling only in occasional flakes.

I felt the need to shake off the immense torpor that was weighing down upon us all and, with an enormous effort, I managed to get out a few words.

"Tomorrow is Christmas!"

Ding!... The wall clock struck a single resounding note.

The Griboin woman had just set on the table a thick raisin pudding, which remained untouched.

I saw that all eyes were riveted on that compact and inedible confection.

Ding!... the clock continued.

The pudding occupied the center of a large platter made of dull pewter, decorated with sizable figurines; my gaze was concentrated on one of them.

The platter had often appeared on the table at dessert time and had never drawn my particular attention (nor, I suppose, that of the others); yet at that moment it seemed to have become the center of an anguished preoccupation, the reason for which I was vainly seeking to establish.

Ding! . . . The third stroke of three o'clock was sounding: it let loose the attack of the obscure forces pent up in Malpertuis.

Ah! . . . was it a sigh or a death rattle that burst from all those throats gripped in the vice of terror?

A sigh of relief faced with something at last become tangible?

A death rattle faced with the first manifestation of hellish laughter? The figurine detached itself from the platter.

I saw a tiny human form, solid and heavy, as if made of pewter or lead; its face, for all that it was no larger than one of the dice of a boudoir gaming set, was so hideous as to be an offense to the very sense of sight. Its arms raised in a gesture of insane rage, it ran over the tablecloth in the direction of Philarète, and I saw that one of its hands was missing.

The taxidermist sat motionless, his eyes starting from his head and his mouth open in a frenzied cry that remained unuttered.

The hideous grotesque had all but reached Philarète when a gigantic hand smashed down upon it.

I heard a sickening sound, like that of an egg being crushed, and a purple stain spread over the whiteness of the linen.

The formidable, retributive hand withdrew and was swallowed up in the folds of a capacious dress, that of Eléonore Cormélon.

Sambucus broke into a peal of frenetic laughter, which convulsed his whole wasted body.

"Well done!" he cackled in a breathless outburst that brought foam to his lips.

"Shut him up, Griboin!" a dreadful voice commanded. And I saw Rosalie Cormélon stretch out a hand as large and as terrible as that of her elder sister.

"The fact is he's not one of us!" the voice continued.

The gnarled figure of Griboin detached itself from among the shadows along the wall.

I saw him lean over, open his mouth, and *blow a jet of red flames* over the small, contorted body of the doctor . . . then, on the leather chair, all that was left was a strange form of smoking ashes.

I began to howl at the top of my voice.

"It's a dream, a nightmare . . . For the love of God let me wake up!"

A fantastic tidal wave caught up everything about me; the forms that surrounded me melted together, rolled one over the other. The three Cormélon sisters, united in a dense mass of veils, hurdled through space like a thick ball of black fog in which there stirred a swam of indistinct horrors. For a few seconds I saw the livid and suppliant visage of Cousin Philarète, immediately replaced by that of Aunt Sylvie, placid and sleeping; then, phosphorescent, the head of Griboin burst forth.

Suddenly I felt myself seized by the hair and hauled violently backwards.

When I had regained possession of my wits I was running through the great hallway of the house at the side of Cousin Philarète.

"Quick, quick," he whispered breathlessly, "to the shop . . . We can still hold out there."

"But what's happening?" I begged. "Oh, Cousin, tell me we're just having a terrible dream."

"God knows," he groaned, pushing open the door of the old shop.

It was so bright there and so peaceful that I had a sense of arriving in a marvelous harbor after the most atrocious of storms;

the gaslight was burning with a fine flame and Lampernisse, seated at the counter, watched our entry with the good-natured air of a man well pleased with himself.

"Lampernisse," said Philarète, "we must accept the struggle, but I fear it will be a pretty unequal one, my friend."

At that point a short but incomprehensible dialogue ensued between the two men.

"You're not one of theirs, Philarète, but the frightful shadow of Cassave still hangs over you!"

"*You* are one of theirs!"

"Alas! . . . but all the same I shall have the worst of it . . ."

"I'll save you, Lampernisse!"

"It's not you, poor Philarète, that will alter Destiny, seated on the granite of the centuries!"

"Help me! . . ."

"Who are you addressing? Those ones? Come now, you know very well they are less than the breath of the wind among the trees!"

Lampernisse had raised his hand and was pointing to the least lit part of the shop.

Three men were seated there, motionless.

One of them was smiling sadly at me; the second shame-facedly avoided my gaze; the third was stiller than stone itself, and I cried out in a fit of wild terror.

I had just recognized Mathias Krook, Uncle Dideloo, and the ill-formed Tchiek.

Lampernisse spoke out in a burst of shrill laughter.

"Just look at them, young sir . . . And to think Philarète takes himself for a god, bringing them back from the dead . . . Look!"

He puffed up his cheeks and blew on the Lazaruses.

A singular life at once animated them. They began to roll about, to sway, to jostle one against the other like rubber balls and, abruptly, they rose to the ceiling and remained pressed against it.

"Empty skins! Nothing but empty skins into which one blows as one blows into a conch shell. Poor, poor Philarète!"

A horrifying clamor arose and I threw myself, face down, to the floor.

Lampernisse let out a cry of distress.

"There they are! We can do nothing against them, unless . . ."

The door was torn brutally from its hinges and, in the darkness of the hallway, I saw three dreadful faces approach, like those I had seen in the house of the old Groulle woman.

⌒⤫

Six sets of steely claws, six eyes of liquid fire, six dragon wings were there, ready to play their infernal role in the melee.

But, against all expectation, the monstrosities did not cross the threshold.

A powerful voice—which I thought I recognized—rang out.

"Noël! Noël! Christ is born again!"

A great chant arose in the distance and I dared raise my bruised face from the floor tiles.

My gaze shifted from the horrible apparitions of darkness and, through the window opposite me, it penetrated into the garden, whence the formidable chant arose.

The whiteness of the snow was picked out in great squares of golden light and, through the leafless branches of the trees, I recognized the monastery whose empty windows were blazing with a blinding illumination.

Lampernisse covered his face and started sobbing.

"The Barbusquins!" he wailed.

And I could not tell whether it was joy or sorrow that echoed in that cry. But I was present now at a scene as grandiose as it was terrible.

The garden was filled with people. I made out the tall, monastic silhouettes, cowled and dressed in broadcloth.

They advanced in serried ranks, at a slow and majestic pace, raising crosses of black wood to the lowering sky.

Slowly they approached the house, chanting awe-inspiring hymns that set the branches shaking like the squalls of wind.

"Noël! Noël!"

Then, once more, a powerful, commanding voice was raised.

"Make way for the true God! Let the phantoms of Hell fall back!"

The first of the hooded faces was now at the window; through the apertures in their cowls I saw eyes shining red with the fever of holy frenzy.

"The Barbusquins!" Lampernisse murmured once more.

And he too fell down with his face against the floor.

It seemed to me that I was becoming very light, that I was floating suspended in the air, that my hands were parting the impalpable, gauzy filaments of a cloud.

Somewhere in an unreal space I saw enormous and repellent dead things fleeing like ships before a storm.

I called upon somebody, I have no idea whom, and for a brief moment I saw the face of the Abbé Doucedame appear, smile, weep—and then vanish.

"All this is just a nightmare!"

It was the ineffectual voice of reason seeking to make itself heard in the depths of my being; but it fell silent and did not repeat these words of consolation.

I was seated in the unlit kitchen; a guttering candle in the hearth of the dead fire cast shadows that flickered from corner to corner.

I could not say how it was that I had got there; at all events it was there that I regained what goes by the name of my "spirits."

I called out, I cried aloud to all that had lived with me under that accursed roof. There was no response.

I was alone in Malpertuis. ALONE!!!

And then I had the incredible courage to set out on an exploratory tour through the nocturnal horror of that hellish house.

The ludicrous forms of Mathias, Uncle Dideloo, and the ill-formed Tchiek were no longer floating against the ceiling of the deserted shop.

I made my way to the Griboins' lodge.

It was deserted.

I looked everywhere for Lampernisse; but he was no longer there.

Cousin Philarète's room was empty, the Cormélon sisters' rooms were empty, and the quarters set aside for Uncle Dideloo and his family were dark and deserted.

A bizarre curiosity took hold of me, compelling me to enter the dining room to see whether the repugnant remains of Doctor Sambucus were still there, but his chair was clean and tidy.

"A nightmare!" I repeated, holding aloft the wax-dripping candle as if it were a torch.

I let out a yell . . . of delight perhaps . . .

Aunt Sylvie was there, sitting in her chair, tranquil and erect.
"Aunt! Aunt!"

Her eyes were closed and my cry did not rouse her from her repose.

I drew close and placed my arm on her shoulder.

Her body slowly toppled over and fell to the floor with a thunderous crash.

It was not a human corpse but a statue of stone that had just shattered on the ground.

And then a voice sounded in the night, very clear: "Now we are alone in Malpertuis!"

"Euryale!" I shouted.

But there was no sign of my cousin.

I ran about the house like a madman, imploring her to come to me.

I saw no sign of her.

My whole being brimming over with desperation, I returned to my point of departure. When I reached the boundary god my candle went out, and, in the depths of the darkness, I saw the terrible green eyes coming toward me.

I felt an immense cold invading my inmost self; I collapsed to the floor and slowly my heart ceased to beat.

End of the first part

INTERCALARY CHAPTER

The Capture of the Gods

> *"Who are they, Thysos? Did I not kill them*
> *with my own hands?"*
>   *"You have killed them in your heart,*
> *Menelaus; and thus for you they will*
> *remain forever terrible."*
>
> —The Atrides[34]

I who, following my theft from the library of the White Fathers—
and perhaps by way of its expiation—have taken upon myself the
daunting task of coordinating the documents in the pewter tube so
as to retrace the story of Malpertuis, here interrupt for a while the
sequence of the narrative of the unfortunate Jean-Jacques Grandsire.

My intention is to insert at this point some pages written by
Doucedame the elder. I have already made use of this material when,
at the beginning of this book, I detached from the manuscript of
the villainous cleric the pages he himself had entitled: *The Vision of
Anacharis.* The few pages I here transcribe are the last I shall pass on
of his prolix writings, the remainder of which amount to no more
than a display—filled with self-importance—of forbidden knowledge, a fearful accumulation of dangerous blasphemies.

It will be particularly noted that Doucedame the elder, carried away by the impetus of his pride, abandons the impersonal to
make use of the detestable "I."

The island belongs to the group of the Cyclades; it must be close to Paros[35] but, for many days, at the mercy of raging tempests, we have been navigating by dead reckoning in especially dangerous waters. We have had glimpses, through the shreds of fog, parted by the gales and as soon closed in again, of the rocky walls of which Anacharsis spoke. He cannot have lied to us: of that I am certain.

Anselme Grandsire came looking for me: he put an argument to me that was very odd for a mariner such as himself.

"At this time of year such a storm is something quite out of the ordinary for any man knows anything about the sea. I suspect that in this case the elements have been enlisted in the service of forces beyond our understanding. There is some secret hidden in this accursed island..."

"No doubt you're right," I replied. "What we are seeking here is nothing at all ordinary."

"Hell and damnation!" he groaned. "Truth to tell I never placed any credence in it... All I know is we were promised a handsome recompense. I never gave it any thought, but regardless of the result we were to be well paid for our trouble. Now it seems the aim is on the point of being achieved. All the same, when one thinks of the appetizing prize..."

I wondered what he was driving at, but I held my peace. His fist crashed down on the table like a blacksmith's hammer.

"Where the sailor gets out of his depth the sorcerer might know what he's about, and your friend, who certainly must be on good terms with the Devil, won't have imposed your repulsive presence upon us without having had a good deal to say to you about it."

"I take it you mean the honorable Seigneur Cassave?" I said quietly.

"That's the name of the personage who's paying us," he replied in an offensive tone. "He didn't seem to me the kind of man who'd go chucking his money away with no hope of any return!"

"To be sure, to be sure..."

"Don't beat about the bush, Doucedame," he bellowed, "unless you want me to throw your guts to the fishes!"

I smiled, for, behind the noisy outbursts of his anger, I sensed him to be anxious and irresolute, and ready to go along with my desires, if not my demands.

"The honorable Seigneur Cassave," I said, "seemed to me a remarkable man. He is still young and yet his wisdom is that of an old man; I believe him to be well versed in many sciences, among them the most mysterious. I have studied a great deal, Monsieur Anselme; I know Latin, Greek, and even the newer languages of the world. Through the agency of their books I have kept company with the historians, the doctors, the Humanists, the Benedictines, the alchemists. Alchemy, necromancy, geomancy, and the other sciences dependent upon magic—black, red, and white—have deigned to confide in me their secrets during my studious vigils. But I feel myself a poor ignoramus beside the honorable Seigneur Cassave, whose knowledge is rooted in the wisdom of the most remote centuries and extends to the arcana of the future.

"In the event of our discovering that which he hopes we might discover, he has armed me with certain powers, feeble enough to be sure, but powers which I am at liberty to use with prudence and discretion."

"In that case...," he shouted.

A cry from the lookout man cut him short.

"The fog is lifting!"

We rushed on deck.

The sea was growing calm, as if by magic; the clouds, fleeing headlong westward, were laying bare the wonderfully blue sky of Attica. And then the sailors began running about like madmen, howling in terror. Oh no, Anacharsis had not lied: and the proof of that is that we lost three of the crew, who died of fright.

⤚⤙

Standing erect on a glassy hillock, one arm aloft in a gesture of power—power with which the honorable Seigneur Cassave had provided me—I pronounced the terrible formulae.

And before me the heavens trembled with fear and, groaning, Hell submitted.

Have we completely fulfilled the fantastic mission?

No, and I tremble to think that Death rises to such heights, and that I have been able to extend my power only over that which death has left.

Ah, how many divinities have I reduced to a tractable captivity, and how the power conferred upon me by the great Cassave has contrived to make grains of sand out of a mountain!

Let us be on our way! All sails set! Let us flee over the open seas for fear that the world of darkness, enraged by the stupendous plundering, hurl itself in pursuit in our wake.

⤚⤙

Cassave has taken delivery of our cargo!

Accursed . . . a thousand times accursed be the house in which he dared, with his terrible sacrilegious hand, warehouse it.

Malpertuis is its name.

JEAN RAY

Let us flee again, though the purses, heavy with gold, render our disordered flight difficult.

Is there, somewhere on this earth, a corner where one can spend one's money and take pleasure in it, and of which Hell and the heavens are ignorant?

><

Caught up as I am in a maze of my own contriving, I must here allow myself a very short digression.

Doucedame the elder has long since left this world for the next.

I cannot but shudder at the thought of the things that that audacious and perverse man had to account for; nevertheless, I believe the intercession of Doucedame the younger will in some degree have been able to attenuate the horrors of Gehenna for that creature that was of his blood.

Poor Abbé Doucedame! I picture him sobbing in terror the day these yellowed pages, written by his ancestor, fell into his hands!

Later, when a degree of calm had returned to him, he must have reached for his beloved pipe and smoked for a long time, in silence, his eyes gazing into vacancy.

I picture the scene that, according to what I have been able to grasp, must have taken place about the sixth of January.

Before him, long processions of books, lit by the flickering, rosy light of a large open fire. All his great silent friends are there, ready to fertilize still further a sharp, inquiring mind: Epictetus, Terence, Saint John Chrysostom, Saint Augustine, Saint Raymond of Pennaforte, Saint Thomas Aquinas, Scaliger ... and, next to a magnificent antiphonary of Saint Gregory, a transcription by Rawlinson of the dread Book of Enoch.

The evening of the Epiphany, dark, torn with wind and downpours of rain, is sanctified by the distant sound of children singing.

"A marvelous evening," the Abbé must have murmured, "when the most sinister humor of the elements cannot extinguish the brightness of a star . . . Will it light my dismal and gloomy way? . . . Alas, I am a wretched man and a miserable sinner, and I have no right to its light!"

He must have taken up the papers and slipped them into the fine leather cover I have before me, sorrowfully shaking his head.

"And when I have at last unveiled what I believe is the true and repellent mystery of Malpertuis, shall I have saved any souls from the dominion of the Evil One? Will God permit me, His unworthy servant, to work for His Glory in winning souls for His Heaven?"

I see Doucedame the younger falling into a troubled reverie, the fire slowly dying in the hearth and the friendly, smiling glow of the books fading in the darkness.

JEAN RAY

PART II: EURYALE

7

The Call of Malpertuis

*Is it sleep or waking that has brought me
the truth?*

—Madame Blavatsky[36]

*The witches of the mountains of Thessaly
used to preserve beautiful living eyes for
seven months in silver urns; then they
would use them as adornments which, for
seven years, would weep pearls.*

—Wickstead, *The Grimoire*[37]

*After these sheets of paper from the hand of Doucedame the elder,
which the reader has just perused and which no doubt will have cast
some light in the surrounding darkness, I here juxtapose the continuation of the memoirs of Jean-Jacques Grandsire.*

I was awakened by a distant sound, like that of a giant's breathing.

I did not recognize the room; it was very white, with walls
like hoarfrost and little shining windows like mother-of-pearl.

It was warm there, warm as the interior of a goldfinch's nest
into which, when the eggs are there, one thrusts a finger; a bright
fire was flickering behind the bars of a slow-burning stove.

Steps sounded in the neighboring room and, as I half-shut my eyes, I saw an unknown woman enter, ruddy-featured and glowing with rude health. She did not remain long, picked up a saucer from the table, polished off the sticky remains of a half-empty cup and left, her enormous backside momentarily blocking the doorway, greedily obstructing it.

The image occurred to me of a ship's figurehead on which, in an access of boyish humor, was inscribed with some charming name that would have redeemed that weight of lard.

Outside, close to the window, a curious, plangent aerial dispute exploded; I raised my head a little and saw the blue sky, frothy with little clouds, like a doll's washing tub, boisterous with darting forms.

"Gulls!" I cried.

And immediately I added:

"The sea!"

The sea lay like a band of steel along the horizon, plumed with distant wisps of smoke.

"Come and look!" I cried again, not knowing to whom I was addressing myself.

I became aware that the rooms surrounding my own were suddenly alive with a confusion of voices; and then, instantly, they fell silent: a door slammed, and I heard another voice—this time, one that was familiar.

"God in heaven! . . . He's recovered!"

A hurricane of petticoats fluttered into the room; sinewy arms embraced me; damp kisses moistened my cheeks.

"Jean-Jacques . . . Monsieur Jean-Jacques . . . Jiji . . . Oh! I should never have left you!"

Elodie was there, sobbing, vibrating like a joyful harp.

"I knew the good Lord would bring you back to me!"

But I remained silent, struck dumb by a great stupor.

Elodie had had a vigorous growth of hair, which she wore drawn tightly back about her head in thick, blacking-dark swathes; and now it was a silvery helmet I saw lying against my chest.

"Elodie—what's happened to us?"

She must have understood me, for her lips puckered in displeasure.

"Nothing, my little one, nothing you need ever remember. Listen ... we've gotten lucky. There's a good doctor living hereabouts. His name's Mandrix. He's coming to see you; and he'll certainly cure you."

"Cure me? But I'm not ill, am I?"

Elodie looked at me with a puzzled expression and looked away.

"You'll have a little ... difficulty walking."

I tried to move my legs ... My God! They were heavy as lead and did not respond to my will.

Elodie must have noticed the painful discovery for she shook her head vigorously.

"I'm telling you, he'll cure you ... Oh, he's very clever. He's traveled a great deal, he was once in the Navy. He knew Nicolas ... your father."

Out of pity for her distress I changed the subject of the conversation and asked where we were.

She grew calmer and began to talk volubly, something I was not accustomed to from her.

We were in the north, close to the sea, in a house hidden away among the dunes: in the evening one could see a lighthouse beam picking out the ships bound for far-off lands.

The fat woman was called Katie; she weighed nearly sixteen stone and carried out the housework as if it were a labor of love.

There was a little seaside town a couple of miles away, built of multicolored little stones. We would take the air there . . . yes, we would, in a little cab, until such time as I regained the use of my limbs, perhaps I'd only need a cane, because Doctor Mandrix was really very good. We would have mussel soup, and French bread rolls with an eel salad, an absolutely marvelous dish!

A fisherman came in, bringing six magnificent soles for the kitchen.

There was a feast in the offing, for Katie would depart for town in a fisherman's cart and bring back liqueurs and a host of other good things. For we must feast, and feast again . . .

But why?

But of course . . . my cure, or at all events my convalescence, what else?

A dreary lassitude took hold of me; Elodie's unaccustomed light-heartedness, that *volte-face* after her calm and austere bearing, the quiet and luminous atmosphere of my room, the breathing of the sea that lay around us on all sides, those promises scattered in profusion before the child lost and found again: all of this left a taste in my mouth of stale sweetmeats.

I did not yet dare to admit that, ever since my return to life, I had been missing the sharp savor of darkness, of anxious foreboding, of terror even.

A splendid winter sun was gilding everything about me; it hurt my nocturnal eyes, habituated to shadows and to trembling lamps ceaselessly menaced by impure spirits.

I would gladly have exchanged all the iodine and all the salt of the open sea, the effluvia of life itself, for the deathly fustiness that stagnated in Malpertuis.

Malpertuis was calling me, calling me as age-old forces call restless migratory creatures across vast distances.

I had shut my eyes, calling to my aid the night of closed eyelids; I was sinking slowly into the velvety gulf of sleep when I felt a hand weighing down on my arm. I recognized it: a large, very beautiful hand, sculpted in old ivory.

"Good day to you, my friend. I am Doctor Mandrix!"

A tall, grave-faced man was standing beside the bed.

I shook my head.

"You're not telling me the truth," I murmured.

His face showed no expression: but a flame lit and was extinguished in the depths of his dark eyes.

"You see . . . I recognized your hand."

"You will walk!" the doctor said in a deep, deliberate tone. "I can do that for you!"

I had a bizarre sensation in my legs, as if the mandibles of insects were picking and tapping at them.

"Get up!"

A terrific shudder convulsed me.

"Get up and walk!"

This was the command of a god making use of his miraculous powers.

Doctor Mandrix was now no more than a shadow. The hand faded away, leaving behind it a trail of fire on my arm. The inmost fibers of my being were vibrating like the muted echo of the peal of a mysterious bell, lost in the unfathomed distance.

Then I slept again.

I was walking.

It did not occur to me to be unduly surprised about this: no doubt Elodie and those about her were mistaken in believing me held bedfast by an inexplicable paralysis.

I was walking on sand, sand as soft as felt.

It was one of those lovely days January sometimes brings to the seashore, filled with light and springtime sweetness.

A wisp of smoke was rising from a hollow in the dunes, and there I came upon a fisherman's small cottage. As I drew closer I heard the creaking of a painted iron sign.

A clumsily lettered inscription sang the praises of the beer and the wines of its cellars, and the excellence of its cuisine; the portrait of a fat, canary-yellow man with slit eyes and a shaven head topped with a long, thin pigtail announced to the passing wanderer that the isolated inn was called *The Crafty Chinaman*.

I pushed open the door and found myself alone in a sort of square enclosure of pitch pine cubicles, encompassed by welcoming leather benches.

The counter that blocked off the far end of the room was adorned with bottles and jugs; a dazzling, multicolored display of alcoholic drinks gleamed there.

I called out; I banged on the resounding wood of the counter.

There was no response: and, to tell the truth, I did not expect anyone to respond.

Suddenly I had the disquieting sensation of not being alone.

I looked about me; I turned slowly on my heels, so that nothing might escape my observation.

The tavern was empty, but the presence was undeniable.

There was a moment when I felt I had made out this presence, at the corner of the furthermost bench.

JEAN RAY

There was a glass on the table there, and an exiguous wisp of smoke seen to be rising.

But no, it was but a new sensory deception; the table gleamed, clean and bare, and the wisp of smoke was no more than a play of reflections.

A moment later the illusion was renewed, this time merely auditory.

I heard the sound of a glass being set back down on a table and the sputtering sound of a wet-drawing pipe being smoked.

My gaze slid along the benches and penetrated into another corner, the darkest corner of the room. I discerned a form.

The fact is that all I saw was the eyes; they were somber and beautiful.

"Nancy!" I exclaimed.

The eyes clouded over and vanished.

They soon reappeared though, closer, almost at the level of my own.

I stretched out a hand, very gently, in a caressing gesture. It struck against something smooth and cold.

It was an urn-shaped vase of thick, barely transparent blue glass; I shuddered at its icy touch.

"Nancy!" I cried again, a catch in my throat.

The eyes did not vanish: they were gazing fixedly at me now, with an indescribable sadness—*they were inside the glass urn*!

And suddenly a voice arose, suppliant, terrible: ". . . Into the sea . . . I beg you . . . throw me into the sea!"

And horrible tears began to flow from the great, wide-open eyes.

"Leave!"

Without warning another voice had broken in imperiously from the table where I had seen the glass and the wisp of smoke.

It was the powerful voice of a man accustomed to issuing commands, but I sensed it to be more sorrowful than hostile.

The glass had returned to the table and the pipe was smoking; but now I also saw the smoker.

It was Commander Nicolas Grandsire.

"Father!"

"Leave!"

I saw his face: it was not turned to me but to the blue urn in which Nancy's eyes continued to weep dreadful tears.

I heard the door open.

The image of my father vanished, as did the glass and the smoke; a last sob issued from the vase and the atrocious vision faded.

A hand settled on my shoulder and, with a slow pressure, forced me to turn.

Doctor Mandrix drew me outside.

He walked at my side, without speaking, his heavy and beautiful hand obliging me to follow him and forbidding me to look back at the mysterious tavern among the dunes.

"I know who you are," I said abruptly.

"Perhaps," he replied quietly.

"Eisengott!"

We went on our way in silence, skirting the darkening sea.

"You must return to Malpertuis," he said suddenly

"My father! . . . My sister!" I cried in despair. "I must go back!"

"You must return to Malpertuis," he repeated.

And all at once an irresistible force took hold of me, and transported me far away.

I never again saw either *The Crafty Chinaman* or the house among the dunes where Elodie must be waiting for me, or Elodie herself.

I found myself in my own town, late at night, among shuttered houses and lightless windows.

My footsteps echoed in the nocturnal silence of the deserted streets, and I let them lead me where they might.

I was aware, however, that I had turned my back on Malpertuis and I thought for a moment I was making my way to the Quai de la Balise, toward our old house. This was not the case.

I passed the bridge and followed the murmuring waters of the river until I came to the bare and grass-grown esplanade of the Pré-aux-Oies.

A solitary lamp was shining in the distance, at the end of the gloomy tunnel of an alleyway.

I made my way straight to it and, three times, I tugged at a greasy bell-pull.

The door was opened; a cat, its enormous eyes gleaming, made off into the darkness.

With a sigh I sank onto a heap of white pelts and stretched out my frozen hands to the rosy, golden enchantment of a splendid fire.

I had found my refuge on the Rue de la Tête Perdue, in the squalid quarters of *la mère* Groulle.

It was only in my first hours in that vile retreat that I began to give my thought to *the explanation of Malpertuis*.

Why was it that for months—which had, furthermore, with the passing of time, taken on the perspective of years—I had been in the thrall of nameless terrors? Why was I submissively obedient to the pleasure of a cruel and mysterious will?

What had the late Cassave had in mind—who, for all that he had been our great uncle, had treated us like outsiders in imposing upon us residence in that nightmare abode?

In point of fact, ever since the malefic power of Malpertuis had manifested itself—and it was not long in so doing—I had made only feeble attempts to comprehend; and those about me had done far less than I.

My good teacher, the Abbé Doucedame, had written: "Foolish is he who calls upon dreams for an explanation."

These words occur in a commentary for which he had only with difficulty obtained an *imprimatur* from the ecclesiastical authorities; and a subsequent sentence had been angrily deleted by the censor: "One does not ask for reasons, whether from God or from the Devil."

And now . . . now, how had it come about that I found myself in that haven of infamy, in the odious house of *la mère* Groulle?

⤙⤚

I'm not complaining; never have I enjoyed a sweeter tranquility, a more complete peace of mind than since my arrival here.

The persecutors of the darkness have probably forgotten me, as sometimes happened in Malpertuis itself.

I am living in the comfortable ambience of a sense of almost absolute freedom of action.

The quarter in which I live is isolated from the rest of the town by a river and a canal spanned by only two bridges, each relatively distant from the other.

I know nobody here, for before I went to Malpertuis in the company of Elodie, Nancy, and even the Abbé Doucedame, I had led a retired life, a life such as my excellent teacher would prefer to call "an inner life," largely given over to the demands of the soul.

Beautiful and hollow-sounding words, the utter vanity of which I am now aware.

La mére Groulle answers when I ring at the doorbell on my return, and with a greedy grunt she accepts the heavy *écus* I drop into her rapacious, outstretched hand.

The blue and mauve room, kept in perfect order, lends itself to my lengthy and hushed reveries: I would find it delightful to end my days here, even though this place had been the scene of one of the gloomiest tragedies of my life.

Down by the canal I have found a pleasant-enough tavern where taciturn mariners put away substantial meals and drain generous, brimming tankards. Nobody there has attempted to establish relations with me, and I have responded in kind to that blissful indifference.

I except from this rule a young woman of modest circumstances whose role in the establishment appears to me not too well defined: waitress, dishwasher, maid of all work and, as like as not, if occasion demands, strumpet. She is called Bets. She has tow blonde hair and is rather heavily built.

In the evening, when the three or four sailors who remain give their whole attention to some involved and silent game of cards, she comes and sits beside me at a table at some distance from the card players and does not disdain to share the jug of mulled wine I offer her.

The fact is, quite simply, we have become friends.

And, one evening, I told her everything.

It was not far off midnight when I finished speaking.

The guests paid their bills and departed after a brief farewell; the landlady, an insignificant, massively indifferent personage, quit her counter, leaving us alone. Outside the wind whistled and burst in gusts against the shutters.

Her hands laid flat on her knees, Bets was staring past my head at the flame of the gas jet, imprisoned in a cylinder of glass.

She said nothing; and her silence troubled me.

"You don't believe me," I muttered. "As far as you're concerned I've just told you a lot of nonsense."

"I'm a simple girl," Bets replied, "who can barely read the words in my Bible. When I was little I watched over geese. Later on I helped my parents, who were brickmakers, gather the red clay of the unhealthy meadowlands. I was brought up in fear of God and in terror of the Devil.

"I believe everything you've just told me because I'm fully aware of the power of the Devil and that of those who serve him.

"When I was sixteen I was promised in marriage to a young man of good reputation who, they said, had a fine future before him. He was the son of a fisherman who worked the parish fishponds, and it was understood he would follow in his father's footsteps.

"One Candlemas night—as you know, Candlemas night is greatly feared—he allowed himself to be tempted by the Evil One and accepted a werewolf's skin. We learned later that, under that hideous form, he had led many benighted travelers to their doom at the haunted crossroads.

"One day my father found the monster's skin in the hollow trunk of a goat-willow. There and then he lit a great fire of dry wood and threw the dangerous pelt into it.

"We heard a dreadful cry in the distance and saw my fiancé come running, out of his mind with rage and pain.

"He tried to throw himself into the flames to retrieve the burning pelt, but the brickmakers held him back and my father thrust it deeper into the fire and held it there until it was burnt to ashes.

"And my husband-to-be broke into pitiful cries, confessed his crimes, and died in hideous agonies.

"I left my village, for the memory of it had become horrible to me.

"So, tell me, why should I not believe you?"

She broke off, seemed to collect her thoughts, and continued.

"If my poor fiancé had had the courage to throw himself on the mercy of the priests and admit his error, he would have been saved in this world and his soul would not now be suffering eternal punishment. If he had dared to speak to me as you have just done, it seems to me I might have been able to do something for him."

"Do you mean," I said very softly, "that you want to help me?"

A sweet smile lit up her features.

"That I want to help you? Oh yes! You must not doubt it for a moment, but I've no idea how to go about it. Everything gathered about you, everything that hems you in is so dark and so complicated! You must let me have a night to think, which isn't much, but while I think my rosary will always be in my hands. It comes from the Holy Land, and in the cross there's a relic they say is very powerful."

She smiled; and at that very moment three mighty blows were struck against the shutters.

She laid her hand on mine.

"Don't go out! That's a dead man knocking!"

Suddenly we were frozen in a stupor of fear, each staring questioningly into the other's eyes.

A voice arose in the street—where the wind had abruptly fallen silent.

"*I am the Rose of Sharon!*"

The Song of Songs welled up like a great tide of pain, and I recognized the voice of Mathias Krook.

Bets had closed her eyes and her whole being was shuddering.

All at once the singing voice was carried away and lost in the heavens.

Bets turned her eyes to me again and her eyes were filled with tears.

"No, no," she murmured, "that isn't a dead man singing. It's something far more terrible, and so horribly sad that my heart breaks at the very thought of what I've heard."

I rose and was on the point of leaving, drawn by a force that called me to go out, but Bets fiercely held me back.

"No, you won't go . . . There's something else now on the other side of the door. I don't know what . . . but it's horrible. You understand? Horrible."

I heard a muffled, clicking sound and I saw a rosary of gleaming, brown beads emerging from my companion's cuff.

"It comes from the Mount of Olives!"

I leant toward her.

"I shan't be leaving, Bets."

She extinguished the flame of the gas lamp and gently pushed me up the unlighted stairs.

It was a strange and very sweet nuptials; I fell asleep with my head on her shoulder and my hand in hers—which had not quit its hold on the rosary of the thrice-blessèd beads.

~

JEAN RAY

Next morning Bets said: "We ought to try and see Eisengott."

I did not think that, when I had taken her into my confidence, I had laid any special stress on the mysterious role of Eisengott, so I asked her: "You know him, then?"

"But of course, everybody knows him! He lives a stone's throw from here, where the canal turns, at the corner of the Place des Ormes and the Rue du Martinet, in a very smart little house where they sell old and sometimes very nice things. See that gold-colored tortoiseshell comb? He sold it to me for next to nothing. The neighbors think a lot of him because he never refuses anyone help or advice."

The Place des Ormes? ... The Rue du Martinet? ... I did indeed recall the shape of an antique shop I had long ago glimpsed. And suddenly I realized that the shop must have backed onto the house of the old Groulle woman. What was one to make of it?

"Right," I said. "I'll go."

I did not shift from my chair, and Bets smiled at me.

"You've time enough, truth to tell."

"Why don't you come with me, Bets?"

"You're right, why not?"

A group of bargemen shoved open the door, making an entry that was even more noisy than usual.

They had teamed up with some of the raftsmen who convey great floats of fir trunks down the waterways from the Black Forest to the coasts of Flanders and Holland.

They had earned a good deal of money and were dead set on spending it.

"Wine for everybody, and a good meal as well!" a handsome, cheery-looking fellow called out.

There was no question of leaving the tavern at that moment; Bets had to serve at table, and I could not refuse those fine fellows' invitation.

We drank a clear, light red wine, and tall bottles of Rhineland wine appeared on the tables to whet the appetite.

The kitchen was filled with smoke and uproar. Pots could be heard clinking and fat spattered in the dripping pans.

"Let's drink!" the big, hearty bargeman commanded. "Old Nick won't be getting us today!"

A sudden sense of disquiet took hold of his companions.

"It doesn't do to mention that name," some of the company muttered.

The big, hearty fellow scratched his head; he had the air of a man caught out, realizing himself to be in the wrong.

"You've got me there, friends. We've been taught not to take the name of the Lord in vain—and still less the three-times accursed name of the Devil!"

"If a man so much as mentions his name," one of the others groaned, "he'll quite likely show up."

I set down the glass I was in the act of raising to my lips: a shadow had at that moment fallen across the table, a shadow that interrupted the light coming from the window.

A face was pressed to the pane, seeking to see into the tavern.

My new friends paid it no heed and doubtless had not even noticed it. Perhaps the vision was for my eyes alone.

There was nothing terrible about the face—far from it—yet my heart began to beat faster.

The face was perfectly white and framed in the shade of a fine woolen hood; the half-closed eyes were smiling at me, a lightly flickering emerald-green flame showing between the long, lowered lashes.

I recognized Euryale.

With a single bound I was in the street.

There was nobody outside the window, and the street was deserted; but, turning the corner, I saw the repulsive silhouette of the old Groulle woman going along, her cat Lupka perched on her shoulder, its huge eyes blinking uncomfortably in the sunlight.

It was twilight when the bargemen left the inn.

Bets, her duty done, threw a brown woolen cape about her shoulders and signed to me to follow her.

"Eisengott's place isn't far from here. At this time of day we'll find him in his shop, looking out onto the street and smoking his pipe."

We followed the banks of the green waters of the canal, where the lights were coming on aboard the coal barges.

Bets was leaning a little heavily on my arm: I felt she was happy and in good spirits and her presence instilled a great calm into my troubled heart.

"What are you thinking about?" I said, out of the blue.

"Why, about you, of course," she answered with her beautiful, native simplicity, "but at the same time I'm thinking about my poor fiancé.

"My village is strung out along the shores of big ponds, very big ponds that are linked to the sea by broad creeks.

"The waters are rich, but the fields thereabouts are all but barren and have a desolate look about them; for all that, the good White Fathers—may God bless them—have built a monastery there.

"If my fiancé had taken me into his confidence, I'd have brought him there and they would have expelled the demon from his soul.

"If you like we'll go and pay them a visit one day; they'll know how to protect you from the mysterious dangers that lie in wait for you."

I pressed her hand tenderly.

"I'll go wherever you like, Bets."

"Yes, when their bell rings it's very easy to understand what it means to say: 'come to me ... come to me ...' And over the door there's an inscription in letters of gold: *If you enter, peace and joy— if you pass by, God go with you!*"

"And if I enter?"

"I'll stay in the village, even though it might upset me, going back; and I'll look out at the monastery steeple and tell myself that it's watching over you and protecting you."

We traversed a few alleyways where night was already closing in and the doors and windows were already shutting on the sleep that was to come.

"There you are! The Rue du Martinet!"

It stretched out before us, somber and deserted, leading off from the canal to a desolate old avenue of leafless plane trees.

"That's strange," my friend murmured.

"What's strange, Bets?"

She made no reply and increased her pace slightly.

"Where's Eisengott's shop then?" I inquired.

I felt her arm trembling.

"I've just told you what I find strange," she said with a worried sigh. "We've been going along the Rue du Martinet and yet . . . oh, how can I say it? This *isn't* the Rue du Martinet! And yet still I know it well. Let's go on!"

We had reached the sleepy avenue. The sky was clear and studded with stars.

"We've lost our way," she said abruptly. "What's the matter with me? There! There's the street!"

It was not the street. Bets realized as much when we had walked its whole cheerless length.

"I don't know what's the matter with me," she sobbed. "And yet I could find my way there with my eyes closed. We've *got* to find it . . . We must!"

Three times she was sure she had found the place; and each time she was obliged to admit she was mistaken.

"Oh!" she complained, "it's as if we were going round in some sort of a magic circle. I'm lost! Where are we?"

We had crossed neither of the two bridges, but nevertheless I was aware that we had been drawn to another quarter of the town. Suddenly I halted in my tracks, letting out a muffled cry:

"There it is . . . There . . ."

The house of great uncle Cassave stood there erect in the night, dark and massive as a mountain. Its shutters were closed, like the eyelids of a corpse and the porch was black and blank as an abyss.

"Bets!" I cried, "let's go! . . . I don't want to go in there!"

She made no reply and I don't know whether or not she was still at my side.

I felt as if soles of lead had been fixed to my feet; it was only with difficulty that I lifted them from the ground and began walking with the heavy tread of a somnambulist.

I was walking...walking...

My entire being was crying out in fear and revulsion, and yet I was making my way to the porch.

Halting at every step, I climbed to the door.

The door opened, or rather, it was open.

In pitch darkness I entered Malpertuis.

8

He Who Puts Out the Lamps

*His crime, according to the gods, was to
have succored the misery of men . . .*

—Hawthorne

At the very farthest point of the great hallway a blue star witnessed
my coming, and I recognized the heavy glass lamp that burned next
to the boundary god.

I advanced toward it, as a traveler lost in a marshland responds
to the treacherous call of a will o' the wisp.

Skirting the wall of the stairwell of the spiral staircase, I
saw the somber heights of the house, studded in their turn with
minuscule points of light: Lampernisse's lamps and candles were all
burning. I called out to him with all the force of my desperation.

"Lampernisse! Lampernisse!"

I received a singular response.

It was a resounding, slack sound; the sound of a loosened sail
flapping in the wind.

And at the topmost point of the spiral staircase a star went
out.

And then, immobile, incapable of breaking the cruel spell that
held me riveted to the spot, I watched the slow death of the lamps.

They were extinguished one by one and, at each of these
eclipses, the sound was repeated, heavy and ferocious.

The darkness was stealthily drawing nearer to me. The upper part of the stairwell was already inky black.

A tallow candle must have been burning in a niche on the floor above; I could not see it, but its wan yellow light was pouring onto the upper treads of the staircase.

A cloud flitted across the stairhead, blacker than the surrounding night, and suddenly the extinction of the candle was accompanied, not by the sound of a torn, flapping sail, but a monstrous cry, a harsh grating as of scrap iron.

At the same time the darkness coagulated about me from the heights of that gloomy vault.

There were still two lights left; that of a beautiful round-flamed lamp that ordinarily burned in a recess on the great landing—of which I could see but a scanty and distant reflection—and that of the brightly colored Venetian lantern, which gave only a very feeble light.

The big, faithful lamp must have put up some resistance, for its light flickered, dimmed, and then brightened again.

A shadow passed, vanished, and reappeared, accompanied by cracking sounds and cries of fury; and, defeated, the lamp yielded.

There remained the lantern.

I could see it very clearly, for it hung at the end of its chain almost above my head: the tenebrous aggressor would have to show itself if the lantern were to suffer the fate of the other sources of light.

And indeed, I saw it—if, that is, one can say that one sees a shadow outline itself against a background of shadow.

Something very large, a sort of swift vapor pierced by two glowing, red, eye-like points, fell upon the gleaming colors—and they were no more.

But at that tragic moment I regained the use of my limbs.

Only one light remained living in the diabolical house: the blue lamp of the boundary god.

I rushed over and took hold of it, determined to defend myself against whatever entity of the night lay in wait.

Then the cries arose.

Never had I heard such heartrending, such desperate cries, and suddenly my name was mingled with yells of inhuman suffering.

"Young master . . . young master, light!"

It was Lampernisse calling out to me from somewhere in the darkness of the floor above.

Quickly I turned up the wick of the blue lamp and a beautiful light burst from my fist, brandished at the menacing darkness.

"Lampernisse . . . take courage . . . I'm coming!"

Enveloped in azure light I bounded up the broad stairs, four at a time, defying the unknown enemy with word and gesture.

"Just come and see if you can take my lamp!"

It did not show itself, and I was able to reach the vast landing from which Lampernisse's cries were coming.

The light leapt before me, spattering the walls and the woodwork with pale blue and calling up fantastic shadows.

"Lampernisse!"

I all but tripped over him and, when I saw him, it took all my strength and all my rage not to let fall the lamp, faced with such a horrific sight.

My poor friend lay on the floor, which was black and sticky with blood; he was hideously naked and an atrocious wound gaped in his skinny flank.

I tried to lend him a helping hand, but he rejected it weakly.

His arms made a slight gesture of impotence and fell back with a metallic sound. I saw then that great, heavy chains held him riveted to the ground.

"Lampernisse!" I beseeched him, "tell me . . ."

He breathed out a dreadful sound, like a death rattle.

"Promise me this . . . ," he murmured.

"Yes, yes, anything . . ."

He opened his glassy eyes and smiled at me.

"No . . . that's not it . . . some light! Oh, mercy!"

He fell on his side, his eyes closed, his wound palpitating.

Something was moving toward me out of the depths of the night, and a monstrous claw came into view at the level of my eyes.

An unbelievably huge bird, an eagle such as to terrify the stars of the heavens themselves, reared up there in the blue light. Its burning eyes stared at me in fury and its beak opened to emit the fearful cry of rage that had haunted Malpertuis from the time of my arrival.

The steely black claw tore the lamp from my grasp and cast it into the far distance. The darkness closed about me like walls of sheet iron.

I heard the monster throw itself upon its victim, and I heard the sound of flesh being torn.

"Promise me this . . . !"

A weak voice, a disembodied voice was murmuring in my ears.

And there was silence.

Then I heard a door opening.

Once again there was a glimmering light in the outer reaches of darkness: the light of a candle or dark lantern held aloft.

Hesitant steps, carefully venturing up the stairway, were approaching.

Sliding its way upward, the patch of light grew larger.

I made out the shape of the candle.

It was fixed in a commonplace candlestick of green earthenware and was held by a trembling hand. A coarse fist of short and stubby fingers protected the flame.

The one holding it stopped short when the light fell on me, and I heard a grunt.

The coarse hand left off protecting the flame and, reaching out to me, seized me by the arm.

"Come on, this way!"

The voice sounded evil.

The candle started aside and its light at last illuminated a face, that of Cousin Philarète.

I stammered his name, but he made no response.

His great, coarse eyes devoured me with a mournful stare and his hand, tightening its grip, forcefully bore me away.

And there and then a gentle yet icy breath blew on my face and I felt myself becoming light, almost immaterial.

Yet a feeling of stiffness bent me double, as if a wrestler had put a hold on me; a snake wound about my legs and curled its way up toward my wrists.

I seemed to be sinking into cold and very deep water.

><rr

"You can see, you can hear, but I assure you that you won't come to any harm."

The pleasant sensation of lightness had persisted, but I was firmly fixed in an absolute immobility: the least movement was impossible; and in fact, I gave no thought to trying, so sweet was that inertia to me.

"I really ought to have it in for you a bit, but I'm an old man who doesn't bear any grudges; all the same you never honestly intended me to bring me that water rail, and it would have made a fine piece, and when you should've caught one of those nasty little creatures in the attics, you lost the trap whose construction had cost me a great deal of time and trouble."

I was stretched out flat on a very cold table. Above my head hung a many-branched chandelier, each of its branches garnished with a thick twist of wax. They burnt with a tall, quiet flame, giving a soft, golden light.

I had recognized Cousin Philarète's voice, but I did not see him: my field of vision being limited, all I could distinguish was the ceiling, with its panels blurred, and the furthermost corner of the room.

"If you could turn your head, you would see the companions you will soon be joining. No doubt you'll be pleased to renew their acquaintance. But you can't move, so I'm going to make them appear before you."

I heard a forceful expulsion of breath, as if somebody were attempting to draw flame from a smoldering log; and then light sounds, as of something almost impalpable striking against the ceiling.

The candle flames flickered a little.

And then three gaunt forms came into view, pressed close against the beams, and I heard Cousin Philarète laughing and slapping his thighs in squalid satisfaction.

"There they are! . . . You recognize them, eh? The only trouble is that all I can do is make them dance on the ceiling like the empty bladders they really are."

His voice made plain his regret.

"The fact is I'm not one of them ... Lampernisse didn't send me word when he had the chance. Ah, that one ... unfortunately I can't send him to join you others; he's *privileged*—you understand? As for you ..."

He fell silent for what seemed to me an infinitely long time.

"For a long time I wasn't sure about you ... and to tell the truth I'm still not sure. Although I was a very faithful servant of Cassave's, I was not his confidant; but it's been weeks since I've had a specimen in my hands. You must understand what I've suffered. I haven't anything to fear any longer on your account, my little lad. As you can see they left me Tchiek, even though his case wasn't any too clear if I'm to go by the strange terrors he inspired in the Griboins. Well now ... The good times have returned for Cousin Philarète. We're going to be able to work—that's to say, live and enjoy all of life's joys."

I heard the silvery clinking of instruments and glass vessels.

"Hmm, hmm ...," he muttered angrily, "before that inexplicable thing happened that robbed me of Aunt Sylvie!

"Another excellent subject that escaped me, but I couldn't work on a statue of stone, the hardest that ever was."

Once again the glass vessels and steel instruments tinkled.

"And there was poor Sambucus ... I loved him dearly, and I should have liked to assure him eternal preservation. Pfuit! All they left me was ashes. That was a dirty trick; it's my opinion they lacked delicacy on that occasion!

"Come now, to work ... It seems to me I caught a whiff of tobacco, so that busybody of an abbé's nearby. Not that he's bothered about *you*; but I know what he's after all the same, and he won't get it. Candlemas night isn't all *that* far off ..."

Then I saw Cousin Philarète.

He was wearing a long overall of unbleached linen and was brandishing a long, tapering scalpel. He tested its cutting edge on his thumbnail.

"Before long you'll be with them," he went on, gesturing toward the mannequins tumbling about on the ceiling. "It's a pity, but I can't preserve your voice, as I did with Mathias Krook. That isn't in my power and I suppose he too must be one of the *privileged*, even though they left him to me . . .

"But I'm not here to unravel problems. I'm a simple man."

The scalpel was at the level of my throat and the hand that held it hesitated for a moment.

I felt no fear. On the contrary, it seemed to me I had reached the threshold of a great peace, of a limitless serenity.

But the gleaming blade was not lowered.

Then suddenly it began to waver feverishly, as if the hand that was pointing it at my throat had been stricken with disquiet or fear.

All at once it vanished and was replaced by Philarète's face.

His face was lividly pale and his protuberant eyes proclaimed the most abject terror.

His mouth twisted and let out broken sobs and words of supplication.

"No, no . . . I won't! You haven't the right . . ."

Behind me a door opened, creaking softly on its hinges.

For the last time Philarète babbled his refrain.

"I'm a simple man . . . Uncle Cassave told me . . ."

His mouth clapped shut with a sharp, dry sound like that of a lid slammed down on a pot and a strange transformation passed over his features.

The life ebbed from his eyes and the eyeballs dully reflected the yellow light of the twisted candles; the wrinkles in his cheeks grew hollower and filled with shadow, and his brow became shiny like marble.

Suddenly he staggered and vanished from my sight.

A dull sound shook the floorboards, followed by a noisy tumult of breaking, tumbling stone.

A voice spoke at my side.

"Don't look! Don't open your eyes!"

Silken soft hands were laid on my face and closed my eyelids.

Once again the hinges creaked. I heard light footsteps retreating.

And immediately I felt the spell that had held me fixed on the taxidermist's table had been lifted. I sat up and a hand helped me to stand.

And I recognized that hand . . .

"Eisengott!"

He was at my side, in his familiar form, wearing his green top-coat, his long beard covering his chest, his grave eyes fixed on mine.

But at that moment I saw in them something other than their customary severity: it seemed to me that a strange emotion had made them brim over with the brightness of gentle tears.

"You're saved!" he said.

I cried out in distress.

"Why did I have to come back here, to this infernal house?" I sobbed. "I recognized you there, by the sea. You were Doctor Mandrix, and you made me come back!"

He continued looking thoughtfully at me with his great, immensely sad eyes, and an incomprehensible word fell from his lips.

"Moïra!"[38]

I reached out supplicating hands to him.

"Who are you, Eisengott? ... You are terrifying and yet you are not cruel like so many of the others who were here with me."

His chest heaved and a look of pathetic despair momentarily troubled his mask of old wax.

"I must not tell you ... The time is not ripe, my poor child."

"I want to leave," I wailed, ever more plaintively.

He gently nodded his approval.

"And leave you shall ... Alas! you will leave Malpertuis, but Malpertuis will follow you through your life. So it has been willed ..."

He broke off, and I saw his hands trembling.

"By whom—or by what, Eisengott?"

Then for a second time his trembling lips the enigmatic word.

"Moïra!"

His head was bowed now, as if he were vanquished by some ineluctable power.

"Let's go!" I said brusquely.

"So be it, but you must put your hand in mine; you must let me guide you, and you must not open your eyes if you are to escape the most terrible of fates!"

I obeyed. We passed through the door and I descended the steps on the arm of my singular protector: the flagstones of the corridor echoed under our feet.

We came to a sudden halt, and I felt the bulky form of Eisengott trembling against my side.

Faraway in the darkness rose the sound of a wild and somber hymn.

"The Barbusquins!" Eisengott exclaimed in terror. "They're coming! They're getting closer! They've risen from the dead!"

He was trembling like a bush in the wind.

"Are you afraid of them?" I asked quietly.

He sighed.

"No," he answered, "but yet for me they represent ... nothingness!"

A cool breeze caressed my face. The hymn was suddenly silenced.

"We're in the street!" I cried joyfully.

"Yes, but I beg you: keep your eyes closed!"

We went on, side by side and in silence, until he lifted the strange interdiction.

I found myself standing outside the inn where Bets worked. A candle end was still burning behind the curtains.

"Go, my child," Eisengott said, releasing his grip on my arm. "Your peace is restored."

I held him back.

"There, by the sea, I saw my father and . . ."

The words stuck in my throat.

". . . and Nancy's eyes," I muttered at last, as best I could.

He shook his head violently.

"Be quiet . . . be quiet! You saw only phantoms, the reflections of hidden things. May the great wills that govern the worlds see to it that they remain hidden to you, my child!"

He made off at such a pace that I did not see him vanish into the darkness.

I pushed open the door of the tavern. Her rosary in her hand, Bets looked up at me with tranquil and smiling eyes.

"You were waiting for me then?" I exclaimed.

"But of course," she said artlessly. "I knew you would soon be back and that I could expect you; after all, I was praying the whole time."

I threw myself into her arms.

"I want to go!" I sobbed. "Far from here! With you!"

Bets kissed me long and gently on the eyes.

"What you want is a good thing, my dear boy. You'll come with me to my village. I'll bring you to the White Fathers," she added with a sigh.

Her eyes filled with tears.

"*Come to me . . . come to me . . .* that's what the bell says; while I was praying for you I heard it as if it were ringing close by, although in reality it's far, far away . . ."

Here end the memoirs of Jean-Jacques Grandsire.

9

Candlemas Night

*At Candlemas the Fiend, the enemy of
light, sets his most terrible snares.*

—Flemish folklore

*The pages that follow are the work of Dom Misseron, whose name in
religion is Père Euchère, Abbot of the monastery of the White Fathers,
with whose name is associated a certain literary reputation; indeed,
we possess some collections made by him of travelers' tales and adventures for, before his pious farewell to the world, he had been a great
traveler.*

*The memoirs of Jean-Jacques Grandsire reposed for many years
in the archives of that virtuous man, and it is only doing justice to him
to record that he left them intact.*

*However, it was never his intention that they should be
published; it needed the intervention of an intruder without probity—
myself, in the event—to bring that about.*

*Thus the story of Malpertuis, which could as like as not have
ended in total mystery, is continued and to some extent—small
enough, alas!—freed from the veils of obscurity that clung about it.*

The good Brother Morin needed no asking to give me a faithful
account of the visitors' arrival.

Matins had been sung and, as the brothers were making their way to the refectory, the man loomed up out of the fog. At a pace made heavy by fatigue he crossed the meadows onto which the southern gate opens.

Brother Morin, whose task it was to keep a watch on that gate and who was making ready to turn out to pasture three of our brown cows that too long a stay in their stalls had visibly enfeebled, saw him coming and hurried to him.

"I want to save you going round the long way by the big meadow," he said. "It's very wet going and the path is in a bad way what with the winter's traffic. To tell the truth I oughtn't to do it; strangers are expected to present themselves at the main gate and be received there by the brother gatekeeper; but it seems to me you're worn out."

Though he was a godly man, Brother Morin was a chatterbox, and nothing pleased him more than a bit of a chinwag.

The man was wearing a short cassock which the fog and the morning rain had soaked through, and a gust of wind had carried off his hat, for he was bare headed and his hair was plastered to his brow and neck.

"There's a splendid fire in the kitchen," the brother continued, "and the coffee is piping hot. The bread was baked only yesterday, so you can have it all fresh, and there's none better. The cheese comes from our own sheep; it's good, though at this time of the year it's on the sharp side."

The traveler muttered some vague thanks.

"You're a man of the Church then?" Brother Morin inquired, rather brusquely; hitherto he had paid little attention to the visitor's dress.

"I am the Abbé Doucedame," the man replied. "I have come here to see the very reverend Father Euchère, to whom I venture to hope I am not wholly unknown."

"Not before you've had a decent meal," the honest Brother Morin retorted. "Our saintly abbot would certainly have something to say to me if I were to let you come to him in your present condition."

The Abbé Doucedame allowed himself to be led to a place by the fire and accepted a generous bowl of *café au lait*; but he declined the enormous hunk of buttered bread and the ample triangle of sheep's cheese.

"I couldn't get a mouthful down," he confessed. "My throat is all swollen and painful and I ache in every limb. I've been walking awful roads all through the night in the rain and the wind; if I hadn't heard the calling of your bell, I believe I would have lain down by the roadside to die."

"Heaven help us!" Brother Morin cried, "you're not going to be taken ill, are you? . . . I was so delighted to have seen somebody . . . There are so few visitors at this time of year."

"I should like to speak to Father Euchère. As quickly as possible," the Abbé Doucedame murmured.

"I'll go straight to him!" exclaimed the excellent Morin. "No, no, stay there by the fire. Our saintly abbot will be perfectly happy to put himself out to welcome you!"

And indeed I immediately left aside my glass of steaming hot milk and the slices of buttered bread, fresh from the oven, that I was savoring with—I'm ashamed to admit it—genuine gluttony, and I followed the talkative Brother Morin to the kitchen.

The Abbé Doucedame was there, sitting by the crackling fire. A cloud of steam was rising from his wet clothing; his head was hanging down onto his chest and he was having difficulty with his breathing.

Brother Morin was moved to pity.

"Poor man!" he cried. "He's fallen asleep!"

I laid my hand on his brow. He was in a raging fever.

"Put him to bed right away, with two warming pans at his feet," I commanded. "And have a glass of really hot milk prepared with rum in it."

It was done, there and then.

A couple of hours later, when I had got through the greater part of my morning's work, I went to see him; and, to my great displeasure, I found him awake and even ready to leave his bed.

"I forbid you to rise," I said severely. "You have taken cold and any thoughtless act could cost you dear. Get that glass down you and I'll have another made ready."

He pressed my hand gratefully.

"The lay brother . . . did he tell you my name?" he asked.

I assented with a gesture.

"My dear Abbé Doucedame," I said, "I take it you won't be surprised if I say I was rather expecting you!"

He shook his head and shot me an uneasy glance.

"To tell the truth Father Euchère, no . . . I take it *he* is here then?"

Again I nodded my head.

"As you say, my dear Doucedame, *he* is here; and I have every hope of protecting him from the evil presences of which he is the unfortunate victim."

"Ah, Father Euchère!" he cried, his voice cut through with sobs, "let us hope it might be so! But even for a man as saintly as yourself the task will be terrible, if not impossible."

He must have read in my expression the reprobation with which I received such an expression of doubt, unworthy of a man of the Church, for he immediately went on:

"Forgive me . . . a lack of confidence in the infinite goodness of God is the greatest of sins."

After a moment's silence he quietly inquired: "And . . . how is he?"

"There's no cause for alarm," I replied. "His life is not in danger, but his soul seems to be dangerously balanced on the edge of the abyss. He has brought here a young girl who some time ago left her village to go and live in the town.

"In the course of their journey here they seem to have had some encounters which have terrified them to the point of prostration.

"I have put him in the care of our brother who tends the sick and is giving him his devoted attention. He seems to be satisfied as to his present condition.

"The rule of our house forbids us to admit women here; otherwise I would gladly have allowed that worthy and courageous young girl to have remained at his bedside."

"Encounters . . . encounters still . . . ," the Abbé Doucedame murmured.

"My God, as you can well imagine, my dear Doucedame, I've cross-questioned the girl. Her name is Bets, and I'm well acquainted with her family; they're respectable people. She was not able to tell me a great deal. Only she spoke of an apparition that loomed up suddenly out of the fog: three hideous monsters that tried repeatedly to bar the way; but each time they retreated because, out of the depths of the mists, a clear, bright voice challenged them.

"Then the horrible phantoms fled, crying 'Euryale! Euryale!,' and, according to Bets, they seemed terrified.

"The plucky child has continued praying and, rightly, believes that in this way the instruments of the Evil One will be powerless against her and her companion.

"But he was trembling with fever when she brought him to us, and his mind was wandering. Tell me, my dear Abbé, do you know anything of this matter?"

"I fear I do," he replied in a dark, muffled tone.

I went on.

"Bets brought me a roll of papers, saying that her friend spent three days and nights writing them. She had neither the time nor the curiosity to read them, but she was sure I would find in them some enlightenment."

I broke off at this point, at a loss as to what to think.

"I read them and . . . how am I to put it? . . . *Those whom God wishes to destroy He first makes mad.*[39] But why should He wish to lay low that poor lad whom such dark powers were hounding? Yet, truth be told, Doucedame, it would be a great weight off my mind if I were certain these pages were the work of a madman . . ."

"*That* he is not!" Doucedame declared forcefully.

"I feared as much," I said. "And may God protect him!"

"You must let me see these writings," the Abbé demanded.

"I should be very willing to, my dear friend, provided you feel strong enough to read them: you must not forget you are a sick man."

"Not *that* sick," he insisted. "What's more, Father Euchère, the reason I have come here is that every fiber of my being cries out to me that time is precious."

"You may well be right," I said after some moments of reflection. "I'm going to turn the papers over to you; may it be granted you to shed some light on this accumulation of darkness!"

I went to see him the next day at noon, when the brother cook had brought him a lenitive broth, which, however, he hardly touched.

"You've read it?" I asked, my throat tight with anxiety.

The Abbé Doucedame looked up at me, his eyes wide with terror.

"I've read it ... Ah, Father Euchère, my young friend was not lying! Every word of it is horribly true."

"The Lord have mercy on all of us!" I cried. "God cannot permit such an abomination!"

The Abbé passed a hand over his sweat-dappled brow.

"I must pull myself together, I must reflect; I need to relate things, one to another, and then I would hope, as you wish, to be able to shed a little light. But for the moment ..."

He hesitated; and his hesitation was visible.

"I have a request to make, an enormous service I should like to ask of you, though it may seem incomprehensible. It concerns a matter—a matter that, unfortunately, is personal ... something terrifying."

"Tell me," I said. "Everything that is in my power or the power of my house will be done."

"Today," he said in a barely audible voice, "is set down in the calendar as ..."

"Today is the last day of January, the day set aside for the celebration of Saint Marcella, who was born in Rome in the year 350 and died at the beginning of the next century. Her life, which was highly edifying, is unfortunately little known and, deeply though I may deplore the fact, the hagiographies tell us very little about her."

"Tomorrow ..." the Abbé Doucedame continued, his eyes fixed on emptiness.

"The day of the purification; we are already preparing to celebrate it with due ceremony, the next day: Candlemas!"

"Candlemas!" the sick man exclaimed. "Yes, yes, I understand: Candlemas!"

"On that day it is the general custom to begin a novena. As you'll be well aware, novenas are most efficacious. In the villages they light holy candles—and they cook waffles, *crêpes*, and cream cakes, the greater part of which find their way into the monastery. In fact, on that day many a hare, caught in a snare, and any number of unfortunate rabbits end up in the pot, not to speak of chickens and ducks.

"This festival always fills me with a joy that has about it a touch of the pagan, for is it not a celebration of light?"

"Light!" the Abbé Doucedame exclaimed. "Ah, Father Euchère, it's only in nearness to God that light is absolute and perfect; in our wretched world the darkness clings to the light like an infernal cupping glass."

He was in a state of high nervous excitement, and I attributed his condition to the fever that was ravaging him.

"You spoke of a service I should do you," I said, shifting the subject.

Never have I seen in a man's eyes a more intense expression of supplication.

"Don't ask me the reason," he groaned, "or at all events not yet. It may be that God will take pity on me and spare me the torments I foresee and which I fear are inescapable. At Candlemas ... Father Euchère, on Candlemas night I must be locked up in a room the windows of which are protected by bars and proof against any escape."

"Eh?" I broke in, astonished. "Nobody will be able to get in with you."

"That isn't what I fear," he burst out. "It isn't a question of excluding unlikely intruders; rather it's a matter of protecting me against myself! What is needed is a room I cannot leave, and from which nobody will allow me out! Oh, Father Euchère, how it pains me to have to ask you such a thing without giving you any good reason."

I commanded him to be silent.

"Everything will be done according to your wishes, my dear brother; and now we must focus only on your recovery."

A smile of relief flitted over his features; and, very shortly afterwards, he was sleeping peacefully.

Next day I found him rested, although weak, and speaking only with great difficulty. The brother who tended the sick pronounced his throat to be inflamed and prescribed a most effective herbal remedy; at the same time that humble but useful auxiliary informed me that the prostrate state in which the young Grandsire had been found on his admission had not dissipated: on the contrary, it was now complicated by agitated and stormy intervals during which the sick man was manifestly the prey of troublesome nightmares. The best sedatives seemed quite without effect.

I was greatly worried at this, for the preparations for the next day's festival demanded almost all of my time.

Shortly after midday the brother gatekeeper announced a visitor.

It was a man of the people, dressed in coarse but comfortable clothes and carrying with him a package wrapped in canvas.

"My name is Piekenbot," he informed me. "I'm a cobbler by trade. It took me two days to get here, and it was a rotten journey I had."

"You're most welcome here," I replied, "and God forbid I should ask you the reason for such a long and tiring journey."

"I'll tell you, all the same," he said, scowling at me from under his thick and heavy eyebrows, "even though it seems to me every bit as rum a business as it will look to you."

With a finger blackened by pitch and polish he pointed to the canvas-wrapped package.

"I have to hand this thing over to a certain Abbé Doucedame."

"You know he's here then!" I exclaimed.

He shook his head, and his brow became even more wrinkled.

"I'm a straightforward, commonsensical working man: is it reasonable for a man like myself to pay attention to a dream, to say nothing of obeying it?"

I reflected before replying; the question seemed too serious to be treated lightly.

"There are times when the Lord, in His infinite wisdom, makes use of dreams to convey to His creature's salutary warnings and even commands."

"That's my own opinion too," he said—and his expression grew somewhat calmer; "but do all dreams come from God?"

I looked at him aghast.

"No," I said. "Sadly, that isn't the case. Let us not forget that the Evil One is a fallen archangel and has at his disposal fearful capacities to lead mortal men into temptation and compel them to sin."

Piekenbot accepted this observation, energetically nodding his bulky and somber head.

"It's just like you say it is. Seeing that I have nothing to hide, I'll tell you why I've come here.

"I had a friend, Philarète, who used to stuff animals and kept a little natural history collection. Some months ago, he gave it all up and went to live in the house of an old gentleman of independent means. A matter of an inheritance, so they said. Three days ago, I saw him in a dream—and, remember now, I never dream. Well now, I saw him, and the look of him gave me no end of a fright. He stood there in front of me, still as a statue; his eyes were dead and cold and horrible to look at. Only his lips moved.

"'Piekenbot,' he said, 'do what I tell you, or it will be the worse for you. Tomorrow at first light you'll find a package wrapped in canvas on your doorstep; whatever you do, you're not to open it. You're to set out right away to the north and you'll come to the monastery of the White Fathers, where you'll find the Abbé Doucedame. The package is meant for him.'

"And at that moment I saw Philarète stagger and fall heavily to the ground.

"You can imagine my terror when I saw that he had broken into pieces and the ground was scattered with great, broken chunks of stone. In a dream, though, you can allow for things being pretty out of the ordinary, don't you agree?

"Next morning, when I woke, I found the package in the place he mentioned, and I felt it was up to me to obey the orders I had received in a dream."

Despite my entreaties Piekenbot refused my invitation to remain a while as our guest and quickly took his leave after having asked for my blessing.

Without further ado I fell to prayer.

"Lord enlighten me!" I implored.

Did the Lord hear my entreaty? For my part I do not for a moment doubt it.

The first thing I saw when I arose next morning was the package Piekenbot had left on the table, and a great terror took possession of my being.

I took it up and locked it away securely in a cupboard in the wall, in which I kept certain valuable objects.

It seemed to me very heavy, and I would go so far as to say that, although I had it in my hands only for a matter of seconds, during the time I held it I experienced a sensation of burning.

I made up my mind not to hand it over to the Abbé Doucedame, whose strange wish came to mind.

The evening drew to a close; a bitter wind set the branches in tumult and, as night fell, a storm began to blow.

Candlemas night had come.

>⚬⚬⚬

Faithful to my promise, at twilight I had the Abbé Doucedame moved into a room in the western tower that, in times gone by, had served as the strong room. The door was of oak; it was provided with three formidable outer locks. The one window, high and narrow, was embellished with a double row of bars, firmly fixed into the wall.

While the lay brothers were installing the Abbé in his makeshift bed, a last ray of the setting sun illuminated the wretched little cell, and the sick man appeared to me as if he were lit up in a halo of blood-red flames.

The sight filled me with a new terror and I made up my mind to spend the greater part of the night in prayer for the salvation of the guests that had been placed in our care.

I have an especial veneration for Saint Robert, Abbot of Molesmes, founder of the monastery of the forest of Cîtaux,[40] but I must admit that this pious worship is rooted in a most unworthy vanity.

JEAN RAY

It so happens that God has willed it that I should be made in the image of that sainted founder, and that I should take an unwarranted pride therein; for all that I have never appealed in vain to the one of whom, in the physical sense of the word, I am no more than the pale reflection.

I invoked him and called upon him to be my guide in the darkness and mystery that surrounded me.

Toward midnight, just as I felt able to take a little rest, there came a discreet knocking at my door.

It was Brother Morin who, with two other faithful brothers, I had posted at the Abbé Doucedame's door, with an eye to the unlikely event of that door being opened contrary to my orders.

The poor man appeared to me perfectly terrified; he was pale and trembling in every limb.

I always have a vulnerary at hand and I made him take it. It seemed to soothe him, and he explained the reason for his coming.

"Someone's walking about in the room!" he said.

"Well, it could be that the Abbé Doucedame has left his bed, though it seemed to me he was in no fit state to do so."

"Oh no, Father," cried Morin. "These aren't the footsteps of a sick man who's hardly able to stand on his feet. They're not even the steps of an ordinary mortal. They're the steps of a giant . . . or rather some sort of animal. There are leaping sounds and crashes that set the walls trembling and even the flagstones in the corridor."

I went with him, without any further words. I knew the good Brother Morin to be somewhat inclined to exaggeration, but I was hardly round the corner before I realized he had been telling the simple truth.

The door with its ornate, triple-iron hinges was being violently shaken and, although it would have defied a battering ram, I expected at any minute to see it come flying off its hinges.

"Abbé Doucedame!" I shouted, "What's happening?"

The answer came—so terrible that we all took flight to the far end of the corridor.

A tiger-like roaring, and then a monstrous voice vomiting forth the most atrocious insults and blasphemies; at the same time, we heard the sound of windowpanes being frenziedly smashed.

I invoked the Lord's holy name, and then that of my protector, Saint Robert, and once again I stood outside the door.

"Doucedame!" I cried out, "in the name of Our Lord Jesus Christ I command you to be quiet!"

A demoniacal bellow of laughter rent the night and I heard the frenetic sound of claws attempting to tear apart the thick wood of the door.

The monastery meanwhile was growing restive; doors were opening and anxious voices were asking what was happening.

Suddenly the bell at the main gate was struck violently and, from afar, I could hear the brother gatekeeper conversing at the grille with a nocturnal visitor.

Before very long the brother came to me, a lantern in his hand.

"Father," he stammered, "it's the brickmaker's young daughter, the one you know, who goes by the name of Bets. She's begging to be let in . . . She says there's a devil, all surrounded in flames, trying to break out of the window in the western tower."

I quickly gave my orders.

"Whatever happens keep that door guarded! Stand facing it with the cross in your hands and repeat the prayers of exorcism! And you, brother gatekeeper, I authorize you to let the young girl enter. I shall come and see her directly."

I found her in the room where, shortly before, I had been keeping my vigil of prayer. She was deathly pale and her face, though bitten by the icy storm wind, was running in sweat.

"Father," she moaned breathlessly, "I know what it is . . ."

Suddenly she stopped speaking and her eyes, big with fear, turned to the cupboard.

I did likewise, and my fear was no less great than hers: some violent blows had just been struck from within the cupboard.

I stood there, hesitant, on the point of opening it when, without warning, the lock shot from the door and the canvas-covered package rolled into the middle of the room.

No! It *leapt* rather than rolled, for it shattered one of the massive chairs that stood by the table.

I began to roar forth the holy and redoubtable words that cast out the Devil, for a frightful life was agitating that shapeless thing.

We saw the canvas tearing, bursting open, and a hideous form twisting in the opening, seeking to free itself from its bonds.

Bets threw herself upon the thing.

"Into the fire! Into the fire with it!" she cried.

The fire was still burning in the grate and the flames were dancing about the heavy logs of beech wood I had placed there in the course of the evening.

I saw Bets at grips with the repugnant, loose-jointed monstrosity, an appalling wolfskin given over to atrocious convulsions.

"Into the fire!" Bets repeated, exerting an astonishing energy.

The first flames now had a grip on the infernal pelt and Bets immediately threw onto it all the firewood that lay piled in the chimney corner.

At the same moment a great uproar shook the monastery; it was a monstrous concert of wailing, of roaring, of cries of inhuman suffering, of curses and supplications.

To it were joined cries of terror from the monks who came running from all directions.

"It's burning! It's burning!" Bets shouted as, insensible to the biting of the flames, she ceaselessly thrust the wolfskin back into the clear, bright fire.

Suddenly it fell inert and, a few seconds later, was no more than a nauseating heap of ashes.

A terrible lamentation arose far off in the corridor, and the weeping of a being suffering the foulest of torments.

Bets looked at me, her eyes filled with tears.

"I'm thinking of my poor fiancé," she said. "Let's go find the man who has ceased to be a werewolf, but whose hours are now numbered."

Without saying a word, I ran to the room in the tower from which the heartrending moans could be heard.

"Open the door," I ordered Brother Morin. "All that is there now is a poor, suffering soul."

He obeyed, trembling.

I took the lantern from the hand of the brother gatekeeper and directed the light onto the truckle bed where the Abbé Doucedame was writhing in a nameless agony.

He was terrible to behold: his skin was raised, here and there, in huge blisters and, in other places his flesh was no more than a blood-red wound.

But, despite his torments, a strange joy was shining in his eyes.

"Save my soul!" he said, barely getting the words out.

The brother who tended the sick was, I say again, a capable man. He had soon made ready balms and soothing compresses.

"Father," the Abbé Doucedame said, in a voice that had once again grown calm and distinct, "God will not let me leave this world without having spoken.

"Let Candlemas day at last be the day of light!"

One of his hands fell away from his body. It was burnt completely to a cinder; but he fell asleep with a beatific smile on his blackened lips.

10

The Abbé Doucedame Speaks

The gods are born of men's belief...
—Voltaire[41]

*A woman's or a poet's dream sufficed to
give birth to a god.*
—Sterne[42]

*When once his shelter was set up, when he
had hunted and fished, when he had cut
arrows and put an edge on harpoons, he
hacked off the branch of a tree and made
of it a god.*
—Zabelthau, *Les Ages d'Or*[43]

The lint and the bandages had transformed the Abbé's head into a
grotesque white sphere, shaded with dark about the places where
the eyes and mouth had been. Those eyes were brilliant and deep as
the sea, as I have sometimes observed in the case of those who are
bidding a moving farewell to life.

He spoke without great difficulty and his mind was clear; he
assured me that he was not suffering very much pain and that he
recognized in this the proof of the Lord's infinite mercy.

"Father," he said, as soon as I had taken my place at his bedside, "I am the grandson of sacrilege. Does that make tonight's fearful drama any clearer to you?"

"Brother," I replied, greatly disturbed by a problem from which the wisdom of our superiors had wisely protected us, "I fear you are leading me into superstition."

". . . which is the bastard daughter of all the world's religions," Doucedame countered with a touch of irony. "I could cite authoritative sources which acknowledge that on Candlemas night the sons of priests, to the sixth generation, assume the form of a monstrous wolf. There are those who hold that this malediction does not persist for so long a period; but I cannot devote the time that is left to me to pointless quibbling.

"Doucedame, my grandfather, was ordained a priest and, may heaven have mercy upon him and upon me, was an unworthy servant of the Lord. For all that, the fearful revelation came to me only late in life and in a foreign land in which I was striving to win poor pagan souls to the glory of the Redeemer. Only one man was aware of that fantastic taint: Captain Nicolas Grandsire, and I am convinced that he did everything in his power to aid and deliver me.

"Yes, when he used to call me *le bonhomme tatou*, he was hinting at that somber, yearly threat; and that without any ill intention, thinking to put me on my guard against the hellish peril.

"It was he who obliged me to leave the southern hemisphere, hoping that the Fiend would not pursue me beyond those distant latitudes.

"He confided to me, in part, the care of his children, whom he had left at home, imagining that, being in contact with those pure souls, my own soul would be freed from the servitude of Satan.

"Alas, I very soon realized that one does not detach oneself so easily from the wheel of fortune, especially if the Tempter himself is turning it to his own pleasure and profit.

"Cassave soon found me out and considered me forthwith to be at his disposal—and, from our very first meeting, his cousin Philarète, the odious naturalist, gave me to understand that *he had a magnificent wolfskin especially for me.*"

I had intended not to interrupt the poor Abbé's dying words, but I could not refrain from asking him a question.

"Who then is, or was, this enigmatic Cassave?"

"Father Euchère, I was on the point of coming to that terrible personage. It was my intention to consecrate to myself only the few moments necessary for my confession and absolution. The doctrine of original sin justifies the punishment of the children for the sins of the fathers; but it also permits them to hope for the remission of sins.

"God undoubtedly allows for exceptions to the terrible law of the punishment of the sacrilegious; but still from time to time He will permit werewolves to appear among men. And for that I cannot but praise Him.

"I shall not again speak of myself and of my breaches of duty, except at the hour when I approach for the last time the altar of penitence, begging that you grant me absolution.

"For the moment I must return to the fearsome task I have undertaken: to tear off the mask of Malpertuis.

"Alas! Father—three times alas!—my efforts have been sterile and there is little indeed that I can tell you. I very much fear that, after I have told you what I have been able to learn, you may find yourself plunged into even deeper darkness than before."

"Who is—or who was—Cassave? Quentin-Moretus Cassave?

"You should not be startled at what I have to say, Father; nor should you believe that it is the fever that inspires me. I first encountered him among that strange sect of *illuminati* that was founded in Germany in 1630 and whose secrets have never been revealed: the Rosicrucians.

"So, you will tell me, this strange and inauspicious man is over two centuries old?

"My response is that you will surely also know that scholars and researchers have admitted, unwittingly and with repugnance, that the Rosicrucians may very well have discovered the elixir of longevity.

"Did not some of them—Rosenkreuz for example—live five hundred or more years? And, what is more disturbing, there is much evidence for their disappearance, but none as to their deaths!

"Quentin Moretus Cassave was a man of enormous learning, and a doctor in the occult and hermetic sciences. I discovered a treatise on demonology and necromancy, to which was added a clear and terrible summary of the Kabbalah, written wholly in his hand, which I consigned without remorse to the flames, so sinister it seemed to me.

"He was a remarkable Hellenist; and I believed it possible that a time might come when, his spirit being purified, he could give himself over to devoted research into the eternal beauty, the imperishable riches of Ancient Greece.

"Ah, how I was to be disillusioned! What odious aspirations lie concealed behind the veil of gold and light!

"Cassave promulgated a law which he intended to exploit to his own terrible advantage: men made the gods, or at least contributed to their perfection and their power. They have prostrated themselves before this immense work of their hands and minds, they have submitted their will, they are obedient to the gods' desires and laws: but at the same time, they have doomed them to death.

"The gods are dying . . . Somewhere in space there are floating unheard-of corpses . . . Somewhere in space, protracted over centuries and millennia, monstrous death agonies are drawing to a close.

"Cassave did not travel much. It was enough for him that his mind should undertake great voyages.

"Furthermore, time barely existed for him, if you allow for the truth of what I have just told you concerning his fantastic longevity.

"One day he gave his orders.

"A ship, manned and provisioned through his good offices, set sail for the seas of Attica.

"My grandfather Doucedame, a perverse but learned man, was aboard; the father of Nicolas Grandsire, Captain Anselme, commanded that ship.

"The crew's instructions were, to say the least, strange.

"*They were to find and bring back the dying gods of Ancient Greece!*

"When I say *dying*, I do so advisedly, for the pagan gods are not dead; there still remains a shudder of life in them.

"Listen now, and listen without trembling, to one of the fearful conceptions that go to make up what I will call *Cassave's law*.

"'Men are not born of the caprice or the will of the gods: on the contrary, the gods owe their existence to the belief of men. Let that belief be extinguished and the gods will die. But that faith is not blown out like a candle flame. It is lit, burns, spreads its light, and dies away. The gods live on it, draw from it their strength and their power, if not their form. Now the gods of Attica have still not vanished from the hearts and minds of humans; legend, books, the arts have continued to feed the fire the centuries have piled high with ashes.'

"Cassave decreed: 'Seek not the corpses of Olympus, but bring back the wounded. I shall make something of them!'

"You have read the memoirs of poor Jean-Jacques ... Now tell me, what do you think?"

I raised my trembling hands.

"My God! Are we to believe that they found ... ?"

"Believe it!" the Abbé Doucedame cried in a loud voice. "But ..."

⌒

At this point the sick man's narrative was cut short by an access of weakness characterized by two successive fits of fainting that filled me with apprehension.

The brother who tended the sick asked me to authorize the administration of a powerful remedy that would restore him to consciousness but might shorten his life by some hours.

After some hesitation (understandable, I believe, on my part), I took the responsibility and gave my permission.

The Abbé Doucedame came to and almost at once resumed speaking. However, the former clarity and precision of his speech was greatly diminished, and the rest of his narrative was no more than a tedious monologue interrupted by long silences, the thread of which was broken at many points. No doubt the fever played a preponderant part in this, and I cannot attribute to what follows anything more than a purely documentary value.

". . . They were floating in the air, others were dead and dissipating in tatters. My grandfather Doucedame drew images, sacrilegious even for pagan gods, saying that divine carrion melted on the four winds of space.

"Others still throbbed with a remnant of life, a life which, Cassave affirmed, they still drew from beliefs obscurely rooted in some human hearts.

"Some of them had retained only a larval sort of life; still others, wretched as they were, had escaped utter decay.

"Thanks to fear, which is livelier in the human heart than faith, the powers of darkness had survived in greater numbers.

"A last goddess, naked and terrified, was cowering, naked and huddled behind the thickets: she was the last of the Gorgons, who had retained all her powers and all her tragic and supreme beauty . . . On the sandy shore the daughters of Tartarus, intimidated, were endeavoring to keep alight a fire of dried seaweed . . .

"Ah! Don't you see them? Vulcan limping, the Furies wringing their clawed hands, Juno wasted away, grubbing up samphire to keep herself alive, and even a single Titan who had escaped Jupiter's wrath, ailing, the slave of Vulcan . . .

"There they were, enraged, desperate, powerless before the might of the new men who had come to reduce them to a state of vassalhood.

"Cassave, grandmaster of the hermetic sciences, had armed Doucedame with formidable formulae, with incantations fit to set the stars of the heavenly vault trembling. And, without shame, he made use of them.

"Ah! Ah! the double-dealing wretch! He pillaged all that was left of the life of the gods. Don't ask me how he did it ... His quill pen did not dare commit to paper such a revelation!"

～✕

Here, after a lengthy pause, the dying man lapsed for more than an hour into delirium. When he became somewhat calmer, I had great difficulty in following his fevered and incoherent utterances.

"They were torn away from their age-old homeland ... They were held captive in a filthy hulk ... How? Under what forms? How am I to know?

"Doucedame kept his silence. But the Rosicrucians—and above all the fearful Cassave—were rich in so many inhuman secrets!

"And Cassave took possession of the gods, like a duly authorized cargo! ... ah!

"The gods, or what remained of them, were traded for golden sovereigns or *écus d'or*, like so many joints of meat! ... ah!

"And if I've understood correctly, Cassave's wishes had not been fulfilled!

"The choice items were quite rotted away; he had no option but to be content with the decaying remains of the Olympians! Ah! It was just as I've described it! Vulcan, or, to be more correct in the terms of Attica, Hephaistos, the heavens' ugly duckling, teamed up with a vague, two-bit lesser god. The Eumenides, grown old in their impotent malice. A wreck of a Titan, once enslaved by Vulcan, with no more Cyclops to command. A fancy man, a nameless underling of Olympus, whom Cassave could not bring himself to identify with the marvelous Apollo.

JEAN RAY

"And, no doubt, others . . . still others . . .

"Cassave, ah! The low swindler who laid down the law to the gods! . . . He soon realized his powerlessness when, after that maleficent capture, he sought to give them form and life!

"In vain he consulted the most formidable grimoires. He was obliged to have recourse to one of his cousins, a creature who seemed the very pattern of sordid stupidity and whom, whether out of contemptuous, joking familiarity or some obscure and incomprehensible design, he had made, if not his confidant, at least the heir to a portion of his infernal knowledge. That stupid, lickspittle underling had a strange and morbid passion: taxidermy! It was the respectable Philarète! He devised a species of bladderlike, seemingly human skins for the divinities. He crammed the gods of Ancient Thessaly into these bags and they were then almost human!!

"Listen . . . one of them . . . she was beautiful, the centuries had been kind to her, she was the last of the Gorgons. He handed her over as their daughter to two unworthy menials who, like Philarète, were his kinsfolk . . . to Dideloo, a brainless copying clerk in the town clerk's office, and his wife, a one-time whore from the port. Ah, the last of the Gorgons, as beautiful and strong as ever: Euryale!"

As evening drew on the Abbé Doucedame fell into a half-conscious condition and our good sick-nurse brother administered to him a calming draught, saying that it would certainly help him to pass peacefully from this life to the next.

I availed myself of a short rest but, at the stroke of ten, Brother Morin, who had taken my place at the dying man's bedside, came to me to say that the Abbé had revived and appeared to be completely lucid.

✎

"Father Euchère," he said, "my time has come. I feel I have not told you everything. There's not much time left to me. Don't tell me otherwise; I feel it.

"Who is, or who was, Quentin Moretus Cassave? That's what I ask myself.

"Was he the incarnation of the Devil? I think not; but I believe the Evil One counted upon him in leaving in his charge the accursed house of Malpertuis in which he sought to bring his fearful experiment to fruition.

"What were his designs in shutting up in that place, after his death, such creatures as these?

"I have no idea, but I would go so far as to hazard a risky conjecture: he was turning over the outcome of the experiment to Destiny itself.

"It seems to me that throughout their sojourn in Malpertuis its inhabitants were subject to unpredictable alternations between the divine and the human condition. And which of the two predominated? Is it possible to say? Confined in moments of awareness? I would go so far as to say they did; but I also think that in those periods they were hardly able to make use of their divine powers. All things considered, they forever remained wretched creatures. And, when the long stretches of forgetfulness supervened, they did not even remember that they were gods. They lived in a strange human and vegetative state interspersed with brief bouts of a sort of anxiety, a diffuse consciousness of their true identity . . ."

Here there was an interruption on my part.

"You have spoken of other divinities, without mentioning their names."

Doucedame seemed to have expected my question. He was making ready to reply when a further lapse into unconsciousness cut him short. He revived however, and continued.

"The paint supplier's shop ... it's a symbol ... the light ... Lampernisse ... ah yes! You remember his last cry?"

"I remember: 'Promise me this!'"

"And he also said, '*That's not it!*' ... Ah! I see it! Lampernisse, who wept because they stole from him the light of the lamps, the eagle that tore at his flesh, the chains that held him fixed to the ground his blood had darkened: Prometheus!"

I let out a cry of horror.

"They came upon Prometheus in his eternal agony and brought him back to make of him Lampernisse!" the Abbé murmured. "Oh, what a mockery! Cassave set Prometheus up in a shop selling painters' colors and lamp oil! ... Prometheus who enjoyed a special status in Malpertuis, due perhaps to the fact that Destiny itself had devolved upon him an eternal agony ... Lampernisse, who was perhaps the only one among the gods made captive by the satanic Cassave still to conserve at least a partial awareness of his divine essence ... *He* never entirely forgot! ... All the rest had long moments of torpor and forgetfulness ... The eagle of Prometheus, the eagle of punishment itself must long have forgotten. That is what permitted the unfortunate Lampernisse to carry on, with the aid of his colors and his light, month in and month out, a fruitless battle—a battle whose tragic issue was nevertheless inscribed on the inexorable wheel of Destiny ..."

For a while the Abbé was silent.

"The eagle . . ." he went on. "There have been times I believed it was attached to Euryale, that it in some way served her. Who knows? Ah! I have believed so many things. Alas, I have not always understood . . . But who can blame me? In the end, what does understanding matter? I had a double mission to accomplish: that of protecting Jean-Jacques and Nancy; and, far more terrible, that of redeeming the monstrous sin of one of my kinsfolk."

Suddenly the Abbé Doucedame was convulsed by a violent shuddering. His eyes opened wide.

"The little beings in the attic . . . remember the minuscule Penates, so many; sometimes good, sometimes evil . . . Captain Anselme brought back only what he found to hand.

"Eisengott . . . the Cormélon sisters . . . Ah! you will surely have guessed at *their* identity . . . As for me, I went deeper and deeper into the question . . . So deep that, in the end, I unnerved Cassave's underlings, Philarète and Sambucus, those persons to whom he had confided a few shreds of his vast and obscure knowledge . . . I would slip into the house without the knowledge of anybody there, without even that of poor Jean-Jacques Grandsire . . . Philarète and Sambucus would tremble with anxiety, even at a whiff of my tobacco . . . They were horrified at the idea that, in the end, I would discover the 'Great Secret,' which would make it possible for me to save Jean-Jacques and bring them to punishment . . . To punishment? . . . That is the business of another power . . . My task is not to be completed . . . God, in His infinite wisdom, has decreed that Destiny's work should not be interrupted . . . May His Holy Name be praised! . . . But some small fragments of the truth have come to my feeble understanding . . . Griboin, spitting forth fire, was beyond any doubt Vulcan; but who was his wife? . . . Can one credit such a fall to the Daughter of the Sea, the old Griboin woman? . . .

Tchiek: was that creature not the remnant of the solitary Titan to escape the wrath of Jupiter and be brought back by Anselme Grandsire? ... Remember what Lampernisse said about him ... Who was Matthias Krook? As I have already told you, Cassave himself never knew and hesitated to identify him with Apollo ... *La mère* Groulle? Why should she not be Juno herself, fallen into the uttermost limits of decay? ... Dideloo! His wife! Philarète! Sambucus! I've spoken to you of them; they were humans, humans and nothing more, Cassave's underlings; in a sense the executors of his will ... And Elodie? ... Who will ever define the role played by that humble woman, pious and devout, in the midst of that turmoil of hellish powers? ... And there remains ... *Her* ..."

Jerkily, with a great effort, the Abbé Doucedame sat up in his bed: spreading them wide in a gesture of impotence, he raised his mutilated arms.

"He brought her back in the fullness of her power, in all her terrifying beauty! Lord, protect Your children from her!"

Gently I persuaded him to lie down again.

"Is it of Euryale that you are speaking?" I asked him, trembling.

But the poor Abbé Doucedame was beyond replying; the light was fading from his eyes.

"Enough!" I cried. "What do these mysteries matter to me, or even the light you can throw upon them! Now you must think of your soul's salvation!"

I administered the sacrament of Extreme Unction, pronouncing the mighty words of absolution that open up Heaven to those who turn toward Him, confident in His justice and His goodness.

When I rose to my feet after the last prayers, the Abbé Doucedame was no longer of this world.

11

The Ides of March

There is no law on earth that does not evoke the Eumenides.
— Petit-Senn, *Le Portefeuille*[44]

... and how many of the gods there are that have gone over to the Devil!
— Wickstead, *The Grimoire*

Oh! for a voice to speak!
— Edgar Poe[45]

Brother Morin, who had been something of a poacher in his youth, and whom I suspected of still setting the odd snare, came and told me that the mistle thrushes, which had wintered in the conifer plantation, were growing restless and that the skulking owl had changed its cry.

The sedge warblers were chattering hoarsely in the marshes and troubling the reeds with their nervous flight. At nightfall their curlews flew low over the untrammeled surface of the water, uttering their mournful cries and, when night had come, the jarring croaks of the first silver-gray herons rose to the sky.

Morin looked worried when he told me that the bird of twilight mystery, the nightjar, was more than three weeks early in its silent return.

"It's a bad omen!" he insisted, and I threatened him with a penance for daring to fall into superstition.

But could I blame him?

A noxious atmosphere, compounded of vague anxieties and forebodings, surrounded us. The good brothers were restless, and their pious duties were affected by their disquiet.

Moreover, my own distress was great, for the condition of Jean-Jacques Grandsire was little or no better.

His intelligence seemed to have failed him in the course of the too-heavy trials that had fallen to his lot; his memory was gone. Could I bring myself to regret this fact? I believe not.

He recognized Bets, for whose sake I continued to infringe the wholesome rule of our house by permitting her long visits to the sick man; and he happily welcomed me at his bedside, even though he addressed me sometimes as his dear Abbé Doucedame, sometimes as his poor Lampernisse.

Toward the middle of March, on an almost spring-like day enlivened by the first chatterings of the teal, his lucidity appeared in some measure to return to him.

However, he showed no sign of any fear and made no allusion whatsoever to any recollections of the fatal house that held him in its thrall.

"If I see Doctor Mandrix again, I'll ask him what has become of my sister Nancy, whose eyes I saw weeping," he said.

I told him firmly it was no more than a bad dream: but he shook his head sorrowfully.

"Mandrix or Eisengott . . . I don't believe he is a bad man."

He laid his emaciated hand on mine.

"I'm expecting him ... perhaps he'll come tomorrow," he said. Then he asked if he might see some pictures, for he took great pleasure in looking at the old books from our library which some talented brothers had enriched with splendid illuminations.

In the evening there was a sudden shift in the weather and the wind, rising to a storm, swept before it clouds heavy with rain and hail.

Two lay brothers, returning from the village, drew my attention to a substantial rise in the level of the nearby river and the streams of the neighborhood; and, fearing floods, I decided to post a watch.

I resolved myself to forgo sleep and took refuge in the library, the windows of which look out over the ponds; from those windows I could monitor the rise in the water level if, by chance, it should take place.

It is a long room, lined with books and very pleasant during the daylight hours, but without very much in the way of artificial lighting, which once night falls renders it particularly dark.

At the beginning of my vigil I was hard put to fight off sleep: the sweetness of muttered prayer weighed down my eyelids and I had recourse to one of my favorite books of devotional writings to keep myself awake. It was *Le Palmier céleste: ou, entretiens de l'âme avec N.S. Jésus-Christ*—a beautiful, old edition, which I loved above all because of its magnificent universal prayer.

It was with joy that I muttered that prayer: "My God, make me prudent in my enterprises, courageous in danger, patient in adversity, humble in success. Let me never neglect to bring attentiveness to my prayers, diligence to the tasks I must perform, and confidence to my resolutions. Lord, inspire me ..."[46]

Three times I repeated: "Lord, inspire me," for the invocation seemed to me especially apt to the hour, when it seemed that my voice found an echo.

Someone had repeated: "Inspire me," but had substituted a name other than that of the Almighty upon whom I was calling.

The voice in the darkness was supplicating: "Moïra, inspire me!"

At once fearful and indignant, I turned; to my great sorrow it had sometimes been my responsibility to combat heretical leanings among men of great piety.

I believed myself to be in the presence of some studious monk who had slipped after me into the library, with the intention of fighting off sleep, so as to keep watch over the threatened danger.

"Who's there?" I inquired, for I could see nothing through the thick gloom in which the little reading lamp was barely more than a starlike glimmer, "and what are you saying?"

The voice resumed, on an infinitely sad note that wrung my heart.

"Moïra, inspire me!"

"Which means . . . ?" I cried; this time I was distinctly alarmed.

I had pushed back my chair and the lamp lit up the shelves of antiphonaries close by.

A tall figure stood silhouetted, motionless, its back to the bookshelves.

The light picked out two joined hands, large and beautiful, then a long, silver beard. Finally, a noble and sorrowful face emerged from the shadows.

"Who are you? You are not from here . . . How did you come here? and why?" I demanded, all in one breath.

"I am expected," he said, "and if you wish to give me a name, call me Eisengott!"

"My God!" I stammered. And I made the sign of the cross. I saw him shudder.

"Do as you will," he murmured. "Your gesture cannot harm me; I am not one of those who wish ill to men."

"If that is so," I said, regaining my courage and feeling myself suddenly reassured in his regard, "then pray with me."

His trembling became more marked; quietly he came closer to me, and I could see him more clearly.

I shall never be able to explain why, at that moment, I felt an immense sense of sadness permeate my whole being.

"Unlucky man!" I cried, "would you refuse the divine consolation of prayer? Then tell me who you are and if I can be of any help to you."

He turned and looked at me with eyes that shone like the stars.

"Let He whom you invoke spare you that knowledge," he exclaimed passionately, "otherwise you will never again know peace on this earth!"

At that moment a violent squall burst against the monastery walls; I heard the frenzied creaking of the weathercocks, the harsh, slapping sound of shutters being torn from their hinges, and a torrential roar of driving rain. Almost at the same instant an enormous burst of sheet lightning lit up the sky and, through the windows, I caught sight of the tormented expanse of waters open to the furious assault of the elements.

The unknown man lifted his huge arms to the heavens in a terrible gesture of invocation.

"The storm is coming," he cried, "and on its vast wings there ride the most awesome of forces. They are coming; in a few seconds they will be upon us! You, Servant of the Nazarene and the victorious cross! Call upon your master to help you!"

One of his huge, white hands fell upon my shoulder and it felt heavy, as if it were made of iron.

Suddenly, more blinding than the lightning flashes that were furrowing the heavens, a revelation dazzled me.

"Eisengott! Eisengott is Zeus, the god of gods!"

I expected a furious recoil on his part, perhaps a terrible return to his ancient omnipotence.

But his eyes were filled with an infinite distress that tore at my heart and moved me to tears.

"Come!" he said with tender firmness. "We must help Jean-Jacques Grandsire."

It was far more of an order than a request; and I sensed, despite my disquiet and my repulsion, that I could not but comply.

I followed him along the corridors where the watching monks were running this way and that, muttering protective prayers or uttering groans of terror.

The monastery was trembling on its foundations. Streams of celestial fire, accompanied by a formidable rumbling of thunder, riveted the heavens to the earth; one of the windows was ripped out of its frame and a torrent of black water burst in at the gaping breach.

Twice I was swept off of my feet by the violence of the wind before I was able to reach the room where the young patient lay.

We found him sitting upright, his horrified gaze fixed on the tormented skies.

Eisengott threw himself upon him.

"Don't look!" he cried. "Keep your eyes averted!"

But the young man did not seem to hear him.

I saw Eisengott pull off one of the bed's blankets and cover the ill man's face with it.

"See to it he doesn't look! . . . See to it he doesn't look!" the old man pleaded.

There was a frenzied thunder of running footsteps in the corridors and I heard the maundering voice of Brother Morin: "The devils!" he was shouting, "the devils!"

Eisengott's iron hand was pressing down heavily on my arm.

"When I tell you not to look any longer you will avert your eyes, and you will do that under pain of there and then losing your life," he commanded. "For the present, though, look, and perhaps it will be given to you to understand."

A powerful authority emanated from his words and, abandoning every last suspicion of resistance, my gaze followed the direction in which his long arm was pointing into the heavens.

The lightning was still burning there; a burning, fiery furnace upon high.

"See!" Eisengott directed me.

I saw.

Three nightmare figures, three nameless horrors vomited up out of the lower depths of Hell were soaring in the vacancy of space on wings as broad as a ship's sails. Twice I caught sight of their faces; and twice I howled out with all my strength, so great was my terror.

Their faces were livid and grimacing masks, contorted in fiendish rage and crowned with serpents writhing in frenzy.

Eisengott burst into a peal of strident laughter.

"You recognize them, Father Euchère? The Eumenides!!! That is only one of the abominations Anselme Grandsire brought back to the great Cassave! The Eumenides!! Tisephone ... Megaera ... Alecto!* The Misses Cormélon, if you prefer! They have come to claim Jean-Jacques ..."

Blazing torches appeared in the claws of the winged monstrosities. Their flight drew perilously close to our walls, and I could hear the fierce hissing of serpents.

All at once Eisengott backed away abruptly.

"Now," I heard him murmur, "now comes the struggle!"

Another form emerged out of the further reaches of the heavens. It issued forth at a pace whose slowness seemed to me more terrible than the incredible velocity of the three infernal beings.

It was an apparition of milky-colored flames from the midst of which emerged a visage: but what a visage ... Never had such a terrible beauty erupted from the mystery of creation!

Gliding on great, wide silent wings it swept over the furious flight of the daughters of Tartarus.

They hesitated; then, with one accord, they turned upon it.

"Don't look anymore!" Eisengott bellowed. And, with a vigorous blow from his great, white hand, he harshly cut off my vision.

I heard a triple roar of rage and pain, followed by an unprecedented clap of thunder.

"It's over!" I heard him murmur.

I opened my eyes: the sky was empty and, to the north, all that could be seen was an enormous shooting star, vanishing into the distance.

At the same moment I heard a distant voice sob: "Euryale!"

---

* Here, for the first time we encounter the true name of the Fury: Alecto. In the recollections of Jean-Jacques Grandsire it appears only in the form of Alecta, which is sweeter and more feminine. (*Author's note.*)

Eisengott let out a cry of despair.

"Curse it! . . . He looked!"

I turned to the sickbed.

It was empty: but Jean-Jacques Grandsire was standing erect in the middle of the room, his face cold as marble, his gaze directed at the now quiet firmament.

I stretched out a hand but, horrified, I at once withdrew it.

I had just touched a statue of stone, without life, without soul!

Eisengott's words fell on the silence like drops of icy water.

"Thus die those who have looked upon the Gorgon!"

The world about me blurred into a swimming chaos: tearing myself away from the arms that sought to retain me, I ran like a madman through the corridors, ceaselessly shouting as I ran:

"The Gorgon! The Gorgon! Don't look!"

12

Eisengott Speaks

*Filled with compassion, Jehovah said to
Jupiter: "I am not sending you death, but
rather rest."*

> *"It would be easy for you to destroy
> me!"*

> *"I shall do no such thing: are you not
> my elder brother?"*

—Hawthorne

*The gods, being subject to the law of
Destiny, were powerless against it . . .*
—A precept of Greek mythology

*I, whom the reader of the obscure and doom-laden story of Malpertuis
will never know save by the name of "the robber of the White
Fathers"—and in a spirit of penitence I accept the appellation—have
come to the end of my task.*

*A feeble light—too feeble a light, alas!—will have projected its
mean and fleeting rays over the somber walls of Malpertuis, and over
the still more somber destinies of those it sheltered.*

*Before me there remains a huge pile of yellowed pages—pages of
which I have made no use. It is the continuation of the manuscript of
Dom Misseron.*

There is little in these pages that warrants publication; for the most part, in any case, they have only the remotest bearing upon Jean-Jacques Grandsire and Malpertuis.

It will suffice the reader to know that the saintly abbot fell gravely ill after the events related in the preceding chapter, that his reason too appears to have faltered and that, for more than a month, he remained in a comatose condition interspersed with fearful dreams. Thereafter, thanks to the devoted care of the brothers, his mental powers of awareness appear to have been restored and he resumed the compilation of the account I have before me, which gives the impression of having become for him something of a hobby, for the most chaotically jumbled assemblage of materials is to be found there, thrown together in a disturbing confusion.

There is surely no great point in reproducing here an incoherent study of the "frères Barbusquin" which, to put no finer point on it, gives evidence of mental fatigue.

Dom Misseron describes them as "terrifying and vengeful phantoms enrolled in the service of Our Blessed Lord to combat the infernal spirits held captive on earth by the horrible Doctor in Magical Sciences, Quentin Moretus Cassave, in his accursed dwelling Malpertuis."

This document is all the more questionable insofar as it is interlarded with completely imaginary hagiographical narratives concerning Saint Anschaire and the illustrious founder of the Carthusians, Saint Bruno,[47] as well as absurd digressions on natural history which treat of the migrations of completely nonexistent birds and of mysterious flowers called into being by moonlight and capable of attracting vampires and werewolves.

Nevertheless there is some point in extracting from the farrago the following disturbing lines:

Eisengott told me: "I was never the captive of Cassave, nor one of his sycophants. I followed my unfortunate friends into their dreadful exile of my own will."

"So," I inquired of him, trembling as I spoke, "O fearsome creature, you must still retain some power?"

"Perhaps ... Such power as, out of pity, is left to me by the great god that you serve, Dom Misseron!"

"But why then, if that power is left to you, did you not save Jean-Jacques?"

"Because, over and above the desires and the aspirations of men, over and above the will of the gods—and my own will too—there remains the inflexible law of Destiny! What is written upon the wheel must be accomplished ..."

"Could you not have ... ?"

"No! ... I did all I could for Jean-Jacques ... In the tragic lot of Destiny it was written that he should be loved by two goddesses held captive by the formulae of Cassave: Euryale, the last of the Gorgons, and Alecto, the third of the Eumenides! ... From that double love there was born a fearsome drama of jealousy, such as was known among the Olympians in the heroic age ... When once, on Christmas night, Euryale let loose her terrible gaze on Jean-Jacques, seeking to petrify him and keep him forever for herself, she was weeping ... Her tears tempered the fire of her eyes and the magical power was only half effective ... It was thanks to that I was able to heal Jean-Jacques ... You were present at the outcome of the drama; you witnessed the struggle of the Eumenides and the Gorgon! ... "

"Of which poor Jean-Jacques was the victim ..."

"He disobeyed! ... Euryale was there that night only to protect him from the Eumenides who sought to seize him ... It was he,

he alone who was responsible: he dared to look upon the Gorgon!
... Moreover, Euryale loved him desperately and protected him ...
Remember the fate she had Philarète suffer the day that hench-
man of Cassave's raised a hand against him? ... Without her the
Eumenides would long since have punished him for his crime ..."

"For his crime ... ?"

"Was he not fated to arouse the love of a goddess, he who was
not himself one of the gods? ... Do you not remember what happened to Uncle Dideloo, who thought he could compel the love of
one of the daughters of Tartarus? ... From time to time the gods
bow before the transgressions of men armed with stolen powers,
but the hour of punishment always comes ... Your great God has
left us that power ... Dideloo! ... Philarète! ... The woman Sylvie,
who imposed her maternal despotism on the last of the Gorgons!
... Sambucus! ... Everyone! ... Even Jean-Jacques! ... He, however,
was not merely a man: a reflected glow of Olympus shown about
his brow! ..."

*... There is no telling where or under what circumstances this strange
encounter between Eisengott and the man of the cloth took place.
Further on is this last piece of writing:*

Despite the lively opposition of the brothers I have had the petri-
fied remains of the unfortunate Jean-Jacques buried in consecrated
ground, albeit at some distance from the burial place of our pious
monks. Strange little flowers grow there, which fall into dust as
soon as one touches them, and plants of so repellant an odor that
one approaches them only at the risk of nausea; I believe they are
related to the anagyris, an ill-omened and noxious herb.

On many occasions I have seen a young girl of great beauty sitting motionless next to the tomb.

I have attempted to speak to her, but at my every approach she has vanished before my eyes, like a puff of smoke. I have nonetheless been able to observe that she had a black bandage bound about her eyes and that her hair, which was of a burning, coppery red color, had a most odd look to it.

On another occasion I saw a young man emerge from the spindle bush hedge with which the monks have surrounded the tomb; his expression was mournful and blood was dripping from his wounded brow. I spoke to him and asked if I could be of any help.

He precipitately took refuge in the depths of the spindle bush hedge; and I heard a sweet, but infinitely sad voice sing Biblical words in a detestable, pagan manner.

"*I am the rose of Sharon!*"

The good brothers report that large and dangerous fish now live in the marshland pools and devour the carp, pike, and eels that for years have contributed to the delights of our table.

Morin asserts that these predators are serpents and claims to have seen them. But one cannot place credence in what the good fellow says: he is a man of great heart and small judgment.

Later, in the midst of a wearisome disquisition on the notorious Barbusquins, Dom Misseron writes:

He was a tall man and well built, whose hair and beard were on the point of turning gray. He stood before me without my having perceived his arrival, which caused me considerable disquiet. I can still hear his heartbreaking voice: yet, try as I may, I cannot call to mind exactly what he told me. But I *can* say, swearing on my eternal salvation, that it was as terrible as the confession of a man eternally damned. Nevertheless I do recall certain of his words:

"My father Anselme Grandsire rescued a goddess from the malign intentions of the disgusting Doucedame.[†] I was the off-spring of their transient liaison on the island of the dead gods, and from that day onward, I have lived only to avenge the gods and to bring about their escape from their sordid captivity.

"You—servant of the triumphant God of the Cross!—do you not realize that my children, Jean-Jacques and Nancy, were them-selves also gods?

"As such they were subject to the strange potency of the law of Cassave. But at the same time, for the implacable Rosicrucian, they were the object of a dark pride . . . Did not a trace of his blood indeed course through their veins? In that regard Cassave was especially mindful and sensitive. He foresaw Euryale's love, and the union of that awe-inspiring deity and his great nephew took on in his eyes the dimensions of an apotheosis. Perhaps he envisaged enormous future possibilities; but Moïra, which is Law to the gods themselves, alone holds the secrets of what is to come. My children were gods and, as such, they were beloved of the gods! Yet they were also mortals. Perhaps it was for that reason that the punish-ment came about: Nancy, whose eyes wept in an urn, had loved a god of light . . . Jean-Jacques had stolen away the love of two ter-rible goddesses . . ."

---

† Dom Misseron here emphasizes that the reference is clearly to the elder Doucedame. (*Author's note.*)

Oh! How empty, how desolate was my spirit at that moment!

I saw abysses over which great birds of prey were sweeping, and then I saw a giant figure that blotted out all space; and this human figure was groaning in terror:

"Moïra! Moïra, before whom the god of gods himself must bow his head . . . Destiny! Destiny!!!"

I remember nothing more of what followed, if indeed there was any continuation of those heartbreaking words or of those events. For that I give thanks to heaven, for any continuation must surely have been ungodly, and deadly to those whose souls live in Our Lord Jesus Christ.

I shall add only one thing more: I have endeavored to discover more about Dom Misseron, that blameless Father Euchère to whom had fallen the dreadful privilege of witnessing the last act of the last drama of Olympus. I had the temerity to return, under a pious pretext, to the good White Fathers, so as to inform myself further concerning him.

I found out little enough. All I could learn was that, toward the end of his life upon this earth Father Euchère sank into a state of dementia, and that he was removed from his beloved monastery.

It seems it was his habit to construct strange little houses of light wood and tissue paper which he would call Malpertuis and then consign to the putrefying flames of an auto-da-fé, proclaiming himself the instrument of Moïra and of the gods . . .

My work is done.

The last folio of the manuscript has been read and set in the context I judge most proper to elucidate this singular and gloomy story.

For a long time I have remained in a pensive state, convinced that a terrifying love affair was the basis of this mysterious drama: one of the Eumenides and a Gorgon caught up in a dispute over the heart of a wretched twenty-year-old youth who, no doubt, was unaware of his divine ancestry.

But what was the fate of those who survived? Did they grow old as humans do and suffer the inescapable law of tomb? Or did they share in the immortality—or rather the longevity—of the gods?

I wrote just now that my work is done. It is not done!

I sense that a mysterious and imperious will is pressing me onward: I must find the town and the house . . .

❧

I will soon be on my way.

Before setting off on this expedition, which fills me with more trepidation than any other in my adventurous career, I have once again read over the pages of this maleficent narrative and put the final touches to their coordination. It is only right that all should be properly in order, in the event that . . .

The years have yellowed the pages of the written account, and time must have done its work on the stones of the town.

But have the gods survived?

End of the second part

EPILOGUE

The Boundary God

*Concerning the gods that are deaf,
although properly provided with ears . . .*
—Jean de la Fontaine[48]

*Tell me the last secret of Huckebrecht, and
free me, free me from the miasmas of this
miserable place of torment.*
—Hermann Esswein,
Der Gespensterfritz[49]

I have found the town!

*I arrived here one evening, by the most modern means of
transport.*

It was late, and the houses were sleeping in the moonlight.

*The atmosphere, though, did not seem to me to have changed
greatly: a drizzle of rain was falling; the light was dim and pallid;
the passersby were few; some new buildings stood out here and there in
contrast to their archaic surroundings, which proclaimed their obstinate attachment to the past.*

*The last doors were being shut, and the shutters were closed on
deep, provincial drowsiness.*

*Nevertheless, I found a tavern. Its windows glowed rosy and the
scent of a tempting roast filtered out through the half-open door.*

I could hear laughter, snatches of song and the alluring clatter of crockery.

I entered, encouraged by the good humor that seemed to reign supreme on the other side of the door.

The company I encountered there was cheerful, heartily doing justice to a copious spread, and warmly welcoming to a stranger.

The cooks went out of their way to prepare for me the best they could provide, and with the meal I enjoyed old wines, the best years of illustrious vineyards.

In a corner of the dining room, at a little table, the waitress would from time to time set down the remains of a terrine and a half-emptied bottle before an old couple who devoured everything that came their way.

My companions of the evening had reached a state of drunkenness bordering upon stupefaction and the conversation had gotten as slow as the fall of a plumb line into the depths; I turned my attention to the ravenous couple.

The man must have once been a veritable giant, but now his shoulders were so bent as to render him hideously humpbacked; as to the woman, she was so ugly as to force the beholder to look away.

She had just spread out on the table an indescribably filthy handkerchief and was in the act of wrapping up some scraps in it.

"Don't do that . . ." the old man grumbled.

His companion shook her head angrily.

"It's for Lupka . . . you never give her a thought . . . Ah, what do you ever give a thought to, you old brute!"

"Keep your mouth shut!" he responded menacingly.

"Hush, hush, my lovely," the shrew chuckled mirthlessly. "Don't you go on thinking you're somebody!"

I caught the eye of the waitress and asked who the strange couple were to whom she was giving her charity.

The amiable girl shrugged her shoulders in a gesture of helpless pity.

"He's an old traveling clockmaker who goes from fair to fair; he's still pretty capable, and he's just been repairing our watches and clocks: so, for a few days we give them bed and board."

"Heh, heh . . ." the old woman continued, "I suppose you're thinking about that beautiful, stuck-up female with the dark eyes? Ha! I tore them out of her head and put them in on old jar!"

"Keep your mouth shut," the wretched old man repeated.

"Ha!" the hag shouted suddenly. "In the old days when . . . aha . . . she would've been turned into a cow! Io! you remember . . . Like Io!"

There was the sound of a blow, sharp and hard, followed by cries of rage and pain.

This time the waitress got angry.

"Oh no! If beggars get to fighting and quarreling . . . Out you get, the pair of you, and don't show yourselves here again!"

The old man got to his feet without a word of protest, dragging his trembling companion after him.

I could hear her in the street, raising her voice in one last complaint.

"And to think I hadn't finished my mutton stew!"

~~~

Three days later I found Malpertuis.

I was aided in my search by the allusion made by Jean-Jacques Grandsire to certain old and rebarbative engravings.

Malpertuis stood before me, dark and hostile, in all the menacing moroseness of its locked doors and closed shutters.

The lock was not complicated and needed little persuasion.

I found the great entrance hall, the yellow drawing room, and various other rooms, just as they had been described.

The boundary god was in his place; I examined him, with no evil intent.

But damn it! . . . even dead gods have a way of leading mortal men into temptation.

It was a rare piece—and I think I know what I'm talking about—of a provenance worthy of the mutilated Venus de Milo!

I was wearing a roomy English greatcoat which more than once in my hardworking existence has stood me in good stead; it served me to perfection to wrap up the solitary divinity, the symbol of the rural honesty of the great classical past.

This windfall had its own effect on my curiosity; I decided to show myself to be suitably noble and generous to Malpertuis and, in exchange for my find, to render it unto its mystery, when the sounds of furtive footsteps drew my attention.

In the course of my career I have made a close study of the sound of footsteps heard in sleeping households, in much the same way as detectives have studied the ashes of pipes and cigars.

There is no difficulty in distinguishing the tread of the person who is on guard and aware of an intruder, from that of another who advances unperturbed.

Despite that, it was difficult for me to classify the footsteps that were making their cautious way toward me through the gray dimness of the surrounding gloom.

My calling—yes, I am obliged to call it to witness—my calling has of necessity given me the faculty of night vision.

JEAN RAY

For me there is no such thing as total darkness: it was all the easier, then, for me to make use of the darkness of Malpertuis to provide myself with the means of defense or of flight.

I made myself a shadow among the shadows, the more readily to reach the door by which I might escape.

The footsteps were descending the staircase with the air of unconcern one attributes to a person who is in no way at pains to make a secret of their coming.

All at once I stopped short, dumbfounded.

The sound was on my left; and yet I saw the staircase to my right.

But immediately I saw the reason: the staircase, whose stout and massive banister rail I could see, was reflected in a huge mirror set in the wall to the right.

And it was in the mirror that the horror appeared to me.

A claw of gleaming steel was sliding down the banister rail; another joined it; and then two vast wings spread.

I saw a creature of great beauty, but terrible as God, bend over and remain immobile in the darkness.

Suddenly the eyes took fire, green as the flares of a monstrous lucifer match.

A nameless agony drilled into my being; my limbs became ice cold, heavy as lead . . .

Yet I could still move, still grope my way along the wall, though it was beyond my power to turn my eyes away from those horrible, moonlike eyes gleaming in the mirror.

But slowly the power of that deadly spell waned; the eyes lost their iridescent ferocity and I saw that they were weeping great moonlight-colored tears.

I reached the door and escaped from the tomb.

The sale of the bust of the boundary god brought me a fortune . . . really, a fortune.

A quarter of the takings sufficed to repurchase the parchment manuscripts, the incunabula, and the antiphonaries I had stolen from the White Fathers.

Tomorrow I shall return to them their property, whilst requesting their prayers . . . and those not for myself alone.

But I shall be keeping the memoir.

They owe me that much.

END

EDITOR'S NOTES

1. Jules Stéphane was the *nom de plume* of Belgian author Jules Watelet (1908–1979). Together with a financier from Antwerp known as Koch, he cofounded Auteurs Associés (Associated Authors), the same press responsible for *Malpertuis* and several of Jean Ray's other key works, as well as books by Stanislas-André Steeman and Thomas Owen (Gérard Bertot). Stéphane's early work, all under other pseudonyms, has been utterly forgotten, but he published a number of novels with Auteurs Associés during the occupation, Including *Le Fils du Président* (1942), *La Bâtisseur* (1943), *Le Boss* (1943), and *Skating* (1943). The *roman policier* or detective novel was his *métier*. Unlike Jean Ray, Stéphane never experienced a revival, and his books remain obscure and out of print.

2. Stanislas-André Steeman (1908–1970) was a Belgian illustrator and author of mystery novels who wrote in French. Over a dozen films based on his works appeared between 1934 and 1965, including *Le Mannequin Assassiné* (*The Murdered Dummy*) directed by Pierre de Hérain in 1948, based on his novel of the same name.

3. Though attributed here to Hawthorne (the use of the surname alone implies that the canonical author *Nathaniel* Hawthorne is meant), this and the other two similarly attributed epigraphs later in the novel appear to be entirely Jean Ray's work (the English is Iain White's translation of Jean Ray's French). Ray likely sought to invoke *The House of the Seven Gables*, an obvious predecessor to *Malpertuis*, as well as *The Marble Faun* and Hawthorne's two volumes of retold tales from Greek mythology: *A Wonder-Book for Girls and Boys* and *Tanglewood Tales*.

4. In Turkish, *Fena* means "evil, bad, wicked, sinister," etc.

5. Presumably *Anagyris foetida*, the Mediterranean Stinkbush or stinking bean trefoil. Its native region extends from the Mediterranean to the Arabian Peninsula.

6. Author, brigand, philanthropist, and professional imposter Stefano Zannowich (1751–1786) certainly seems an appropriate figure for Jean Ray to name-check. Although the details of Zannowich's biography are as muddled as Ray's, his exploits included the impersonation of Russian Tsar Peter III. His major work, *Turska Pisma* (*Turkish Letters*), first published in 1776, has come to be recognized as an important early example of the epistolary novel.

7. A theorbo is a form of bass lute with six to eight strings, commonly used in the sixteenth through the eighteenth centuries. Adriaen Brouwer (1605–1638) was a seventeenth-century Flemish painter best known for his depictions of drunkards and gamblers. In Greek mythology, Amphitrite was a sea goddess married to Poseidon. Mabuse here refers to Jan Gossaert (1478–1532), a French-speaking painter who introduced elements of Italian Renaissance painting to the north. He took the name Jan Mabuse after Maubeuge, the commune in the north of France where he was born.

8. Orange-flower water.

9. Rather than a specific text, "The Tales of Hussein" appears to imply that this anecdote is taken from the extensive corpus of narratives regarding Husayn ibn Ali ibn Abi Talib (CE 626–680), the grandson of the prophet Muhammad. Soldiers of the Umayyad dynasty beheaded Husayn after he refused to submit to the unlawful rule of the Caliph Yazid I. Husayn remains an important model both of resistance to oppression and of self-sacrifice, not only within Islam, but well beyond. The text that Jean Ray includes here, whatever its origins, likely refers to how the Umayyad troops took Husayn's head to Yazid I in Damascus. His family later recovered it, and it is now interred with his body in a beautiful mosque in Karbala, Iraq.

10. This epigraph is one of the few in *Malpertuis* that we can verify with some certainty. The original source is the third act of the 1881 play *Gengangere* (*Ghosts*) by Henrik Johan Ibsen (1828–1906):

OSVALD: Mor, gi' mig solen.	OSVALD: Mother, give me the sun.
FRU ALVING: Hvad siger du?	MRS. ALVING: What are you saying?
OSVALD: Gi' mig solen.	OSVALD: Give me the sun.

11. Both Worth and *Folklore Comparé* may be Jean Ray's creations, as I have been unable to identify either, but *Glasmännchen* (glass men) are part of Germanic folklore: more obscure than kobolds and brownies, but legitimate nonetheless. Curiously, one of the best-known tales involving *Glasmännchen* is *Das kalte Herz* (*The Cold Heart*) by Wilhelm Hauff, whom Ray cites later in the novel. Both this story and the one Ray references later first appeared in Hauff's *Märchen almanach auf das Jahr 1826* (Fairytale almanac of 1826).

12. King Arthur's legendary half-sister and the mother of his son and murderer Mordred. The number and location of her castles varies between sources, but the imprisonment of Sir Lancelot and the events of *Sir Gawain and the Green Knight* are among the events said to have occurred in one or more of them.

13. Wendel Dietterlin (ca. 1550–1599) was a German painter, printmaker, and architectural theoretician. As only one of his paintings survives today, he is best known for *Architectvra: Von Außtheilung, Symmetria vnd Proportion der Fünff Seulen* (*Architecture: Of Division, Symmetry, and Proportion of the Five Columns*), his 1598 treatise on architectural ornament. Gerrit Dou (1613–1675) was a Dutch Golden Age painter and a student of Rembrandt. He is particularly well-known for his diminutive trompe-l'œil "niche" paintings. Dou appears in the short story "Schalken the Painter" by J. Sheridan Le Fanu, and British actor Toby Jones portrayed him in Peter Greenaway's 2007 film *Nightwatching*, about the creation of Rembrandt's *The Night Watch*.

14. Doctor Mises was a pseudonym of the German philosopher Gustav Theodor Fechner (1801–1887). He wrote his *Vergleichende Anatomie der Engel* (*Comparative Anatomy of Angels*) in 1825. It explains, in a most fanciful way, why angels take the form of many-eyed wheels within wheels.

15. The late twelfth-century *Le Roman de Renart* by Pierre de Saint Cloud was one of the earliest published narratives to present the adventures of Reynard the Fox, a central figure by that time in French, Dutch, English, and German folklore. "Malpertuis," spelled in a variety of ways over time and between tongues, was Reynard's principal castle, a labyrinthine edifice that offered him multiple routes of escape when he was pursued. These satirical and antiestablishment tales became so popular that the name "Reynard" largely replaced the Old French *goupil* as the word for "fox."

16. "Herpeton" derives from the Ancient Greek ἑρπετόν, which means "creeping animal" or reptile, and provides the basis for herpetology, the study of reptiles. The term may also refer to Erpeton tentaculatum, the tentacled snake of Southeast Asia. Although Jean Ray probably uses it in the general sense, it is possible that he meant to imply the specific species, as the latter has been known to science since 1800 and was first described in French by the naturalist La Cépède (Bernard-Germain-Étienne de La Ville-sur-Illon, comte de Lacépède; 1756–1825).

17. The tarasque is a mythical dragon/chimera specifically associated with Provence, curiously similar in form to the Ankylosauria dinosaurs.

18. A neologism created by Paracelsus (1493–1541) for the purpose of identifying his brand of alchemy as the process of separating the pure from the impure.

19. Soufflés made with bone marrow.

20. A fillet in Port wine with hazelnut purée.

21. A dessert of sweetened rice, often including raisins and vanilla, and, of course, rum.

22. Although Jean Ray alludes here to "Die Geschichte von dem Gespensterschiff" ("The Tale of the Ghost Ship") by Wilhelm Hauff (1802–1827), a citizen of what was then the Kingdom of Württemberg (now part of the German state of Baden-Württemberg), the specific passage in the original remains elusive, and the epigraph in *Malpertuis* probably represents a paraphrase or loose translation. The closest text in the original German is: "Nicht einmal laut zu sprechen wagten wir, aus Furcht, der tote, am Mast angespießte Kapitano möchte seine starren Augen nach uns hindrehen oder einer der Getöteten möchte seinen Kopf umwenden." ("We did not even dare to speak out loud, for fear the dead Kapitano, impaled on the mast, desired to turn his gaze to stare at us in turn, or that one of the murdered men would turn his head.")

23. Saint Venera, a second-century Christian martyr, is believed to have died on 26 July 143 CE. The simple prayer translates into English as "Noble and holy Vénérande, To you I make a humble offering."

24. "Canemuche" represents an alternate spelling of *cane mouche*, an archaic name for the northern shoveler duck (*Spatula clypeata*), though a duck's leg (*gigot*) is hardly a meal for a hungry person. Perhaps that is the point of Doctor Sambucus' sarcasm.

25. The verses from *The Song of Solomon* here are out of sequence. The first is 2:1–2; the second is part of 1:3. White offers the King James Version of both verses.

26. Jakob Elias Poritzky (1876–1935) was born in Lomza, Poland, but moved to Karlsruhe, Germany, with his parents as a small child. In his youth he moved between France and Germany and studied business, drama, and philosophy, eventually devoting himself to literary endeavors and essays. From 1915 to 1916, he was the head director and dramatic advisor of the Baden State Theater in Karlsruhe. His collection *Gespenstergeschichten* (Ghost stories) appeared in 1913.

27. Augustin-Jean Fresnel (1788–1827) was the French physicist and engineer whose optical research resulted in the wave theory of light, replacing Newton's earlier corpuscular theory. He is most widely remembered today for the prismatic lighthouse lenses that bear his name. Interference is the phenomenon via which two wave patterns (of light, liquid, sound, etc.) can either amplify or cancel each other out depending on their mutual coherence or lack thereof. The British poly-math Thomas Young (1773–1829) first identified this phenomenon in an 1803 experiment, but Frensel's work expanded on Young's in important ways.

28. The Prudhoe Lions are two monumental sculptures of red granite from the Eighteenth Dynasty of Ancient Egypt (ca. 1370 BCE). They originally came from

Nubia but were transferred to Jebel Barkal in the third century BCE, from whence they were taken much later by Lord Prudhoe, who "donated" them to the British Museum in 1835.

29. A type of print popular in France in the nineteenth century, depicting naively idealized scenarios.

30. Two varieties of French coinage already obsolete when *Malpertuis* was published.

31. The Book of Enoch is an ancient Hebrew apocalyptic religious text. Tradition assigns its authorship to Enoch, the great-grandfather of Noah. The most complete surviving version of this book exists only in the Ethiopian language Ge'ez and its associated writing system, Fidäl, although earlier fragments exist in Aramaic, Greek, and Latin. Although the passage Jean Ray quotes here appears to be either a very loose paraphrase or entirely apocryphal, it is consistent with the content of the original.

32. *Cato Maior de Senectute* ("Cato the Elder on Old Age") is a 44 BCE essay by the Roman statesman and orator Marcus Tullius Cicero (106–43 BCE). In this text, Cicero discourses on the subjects of old age and mortality, and ventriloquizes Cato the Elder in order to lend his opinions more weight. One of its most famous (and relevant to our subject) quotes is: "No one is so old they don't think they can live another year" (*Nemo enim est tam senex qui se annum non putet posse vivere*).

33. The original French is Job 38:2 (not Zechariah).

34. Although an earlier reference to "the Atrides" in Chapter 4 clearly refers to that infamous Mycenaean dynasty of literature and legend, so grievously afflicted by tragedy, here Jean Ray is drawing from the extensive cycle of dramas about this clan. At the heart of this cycle are Sophocles's *Electra*; Euripides's *Electra*, *Iphigenia in Tauris*, *Iphigenia at Aulis*, and *Orestes*; and the *Oresteia* trilogy by Aeschylus (*Agamemnon*, *Choephori*, *Eumenides*). Jean Ray's specific source for this quote remains obscure, and he may once again be paraphrasing from memory. The use of "Thysos" as a transliteration for "Thyestes" (Θυέστης) is obscure.

35. The Cyclades are an island group in the Aegean, so named because they surround the sacred island of Delos in a rough circle. Paros is a large island in the southeastern part of this group, located east of the large island of Naxos.

36. Helena Petrovna Blavatsky (1831–1891) was the cofounder and central figure of Theosophy. Whether or not this specific quote appears in her voluminous writings remains unclear, but it does reflect the spirit of her philosophy.

37. Wickstead (or Wickstaed—the name appears both ways in the French editions) and his *Grimoire* appear to be Jean Ray's creations.

38. *Moïra* (*Μοîρα*) is the Greek word for fate—both one's personal fate or destiny and any of the three individual goddesses who controlled it (the *Μοîραι*).

39. This phrase is one of great antiquity, appearing in a variant form as early as the *Antigone* of Sophocles. The version in the original French, "Dieu rend fous ceux qu'il veut perdre," is closer to the Latin version, "Quos vult perdere, Juppiter dementat."

40. Robert of Molesme (1028–1111), an abbot and a founder of the Cistercian Order, was canonized in 1222 by Pope Honorius III. He shares his feast day of 26 January with Alberic and Stephen Harding, two of the monks who left Molesme with him in 1098, intending never to return. Together they founded Cîteaux Abbey in a desolate forest valley, on land they received from Renaud, the viscount of Beaune.

41. This quote also appears to be apocryphal. Whether Jean Ray fabricated it or encountered it elsewhere as attributed to Voltaire, we cannot know for certain.

42. This quote is also one of Jean Ray's fabrications.

43. Both book and author appear to be Jean Ray's creations. The name Zabelthau is perhaps an allusion to the family name of key characters in E. T. A. Hoffmann's tale "Die Königsbraut" ("The King's Bride").

44. Jean-Antoine Petit (1792–1870) was a French-Swiss poet, journalist, and satirist who wrote under the pseudonym John Petit-Senn. Although the line Jean Ray quotes here is similar in character to many of Petit-Senn's aphorisms, it does not occur in Le Portefeuille (1865). Like Voltaire, he was an author to whom spurious quotes were often attributed even in Ray's day.

45. This quote is one of the few in Malpertuis that is completely verifiable and accurately attributed. It occurs in the final paragraphs of "The Pit and the Pendulum."

46. The *Holy Palm, or Discourses Upon the Soul with Our Savior Jesus Christ*, a Christian prayerbook published by J. F. Bassompierre in 1771. The passage that Jean Ray quotes appears on page 339 and is part of a much longer universal orison "Pour tut ce qui regarde le salut" ("For all that regards salvation").

47. Saint Ansgar (801–865) was a Frankish Archbishop known as Apostle of the North for his role in bringing Christianity to large parts of Northern Europe. Saint Bruno may refer to either Bruno of Cologne (1030–1101) or Bruno the Great (925–965), a ruler of Saxony.

48. Jean de La Fontaine (1621–1695) was a French poet best known for the twelve volumes of his *Fables*, which contain 239 stories from both Western and Eastern traditions done over into French free verse. The passage here comes from the second line of "The Man and the Wooden Idol," a fable in the eighth volume. The full passage reads:

Certain païen chez lui gardait un dieu de bois,

De ces dieux qui sont sourds, bien qu'ayant des oreilles.

Le païen cependant s'en promettait merveilles.

(A certain pagan kept a wooden god in his home,

Of those gods who are deaf, they though have ears.

The pagan, however, promised himself wonders.)

49. Edmund Hermann Heinrich August Eßwein (1877–1934) was a German author and translator. "Der Gespenstfritz und die Regentrude oder as Märchen einer Magierhe" ("Fritz the ghost and the rainmaiden, the fairytale of a magical marriage") was a story in his 1912 collection *Megander, der Mann mit den zween Köpfen, und andere Geschichten* (Megander, the man with two heads and other stories). Although that story does contain a character named Adrian Huckebrecht, the specific passage that Jean Ray quotes appears to be either a paraphrase from memory or a very loose translation.

AFTERWORD

The Gorgon in the Fox's Den

. . . le fantastique est une tête de Méduse

—Alain Chareyre-Méjan,

La Réel et le Fantastique, 1999

Reader, regard the dark heart of Jean Ray's oeuvre, *Malpertuis*, the spider at the center of a wide and remarkable web. Whichever way one approaches the old rogue's work—chronologically or thematically, in terms of its literary significance or reputation, *Malpertuis* awaits at the center. *Malpertuis* the novel, Malpertuis the house, the mansion of old Reynard the Fox, famous from centuries of European folklore. And at the center of *Malpertuis/*Malpertuis awaits . . .

For some of you, drawn here by the novel's reputation and fame, *Malpertuis* may represent your first encounter with Jean Ray. Should you wish for more, you may now travel from this point backward all the way to *Whiskey Tales*, through four full short fiction collections already available in English, and—once all these works have been translated—onward as far as *Dark Tales of Golf*, and eventually, perhaps even outward to the more than 110 detective stories featuring Harry Dickson, the "American Sherlock Holmes." A considerable body of material exists in Dutch as well as in French, including the well-regarded 1949 novel *Geierstein*, which some critics have compared favorably to *Malpertuis*. Or you may wish to linger a while yet over this remarkable puzzle-box of a novel about a remarkable puzzle-box of a house, the literary labyrinth of one of fiction's greatest foxes.

It is very much the sort of work that both inspires and rewards multiple readings, as the preeminent Jean Ray scholar, Arnaud Huftier, points out in the opening of his own afterword to the most recent French edition.[1]

Within the bounds of *Malpertuis* you will have encountered, in varying degrees, the key components of many of Jean Ray's greatest works: a sinister sorcerer, a supernatural guardian, a creepy taxidermist (and creepier taxidermy), an ancient house replete with passageways and secrets, thievery and a thief, found manuscripts, intercalary texts, and intercalary worlds. Although this novel may not be as "weird" as some of Ray's finest shorter work, it does accomplish spectacularly that *sine qua non* of the great weird tale (and something rarely achieved so well at novel length): an atmosphere of dread sustained from cover to cover. *Malpertuis* is Jean Ray's most fully realized longer work, and the one over which he labored the longest: in every regard, an extraordinary piece of literary craftsmanship.

Although most evidence suggests that Jean Ray rarely revised his work, *Malpertuis* represents the major exception. This became clear in 1981, when critic Jacques Van Herp published several previously unknown Jean Ray texts in an edition of *Cahiers de L'Herne* devoted to the author known as the "Belgian Poe." The most important of these was a novella, "Aux Lisières des Ténèbres" ("On the Margins of Darkness"). Therein we find alternate versions of portions of several of Ray's most important works, including "The Centipede," "The Great Nocturnal," and *Malpertuis*.[2] "On the Margins of Darkness" is a far darker narrative than any of these, however; it is, in fact, probably the darkest and most shocking thing that survives from Jean Ray's pen. Its protagonist, who corresponds to Jean-Jacques Grandsire, is a brutal serial murderer more like Théodule Notte, his older counterpart in "The Great Nocturnal," than the naïve and innocuous protagonist of *Malpertuis*. Most importantly, this alternate narrative shows us that *Malpertuis* comprises material that Jean Ray worked on over an unusually long period of time. André Verbrugghen, the head of L'Amicale Jean

Ray, has even suggested that Ray wrote some or all of "On the Margins of Darkness" during his two-year prison stint in the late 1920s, a period that also gave birth to the celebrated stories "The Gloomy Alley" and "The Mainz Psalter."

In another text in the same volume of *Cahiers de L'Herne* Jean Ray himself claims to have worked on *Malpertuis* "over the years, ten years, eleven years perhaps, throughout the nights and voyages all over the world." Of course, we know now, thanks to Jean Ray's biographer Geert Vandamme, that the author's legendary seafaring career was just a legend after all.[3] Indeed, the myth of Jean Ray the sailor was a central component of one of his greatest works: the sprawling metafiction of his autobiography, which some of his friends and colleagues perpetuated and contributed to. Nonetheless, even though those voyages never occurred, that timeframe for the construction of *Malpertuis* seems plausible at a minimum. The novel is the product of long and careful labor: extraordinary for an author whose process is said to have approached automatic writing and who sometimes completed entire stories overnight.

Van Herp presented "On the Margins of Darkness" as incomplete. The original preface claims that a second manuscript, the narrative of a character named Herckenslach, would illuminate events in the surviving portion, much as with the second half of "The Gloomy Alley" and the later portions of *Malpertuis* itself, but no evidence exists that Jean Ray ever completed the story of Herckenslach. This obscure character probably corresponded either to Hippolyte Baes in "The Great Nocturnal" and Eisengott in *Malpertuis*, or to Captain Sudan in the former and Cassave in the latter: either the supernatural guardian or the demonic sorcerer. The name even appears in an early outline of the novel, and its position in that outline (published in the aforementioned Jean Ray edition of *Cahiers de L'Herne*) points slightly more toward Eisengott. As the notebooks from which Van Herp obtained these texts have since been lost, we likely know all we ever will about this story.

We do know from the published version that the original story was much more explicitly sexual and transgressive than the later narratives—more so than anything else Jean Ray published during his lifetime, for that matter. "On the Margins of Darkness" also contained a touch of the anti-Semitism that mars the author's first collection, *Whiskey Tales*, though it mostly disappears from his later works (and after his two-year prison stint). This suggests that his first attempts to tell some form of this story began as far back as the 1920s, just as Verbrugghen has suggested. It may be important to note that the anti-Semitic elements of this posthumously published novella occur in sections that reappear later in *Malpertuis* and "The Centipede," but that in those texts these troublesome elements are completely absent. Although the Jewish character from the novella remains in the latter story, he is presented as courageous and wise, even heroic. In *Malpertuis* he clearly corresponds to Eisengott, arguably the novel's most noble character.[4]

Thus, it seems that *Malpertuis* represents a tale Jean Ray sought to tell for as long as two decades before finally succeeding to his satisfaction. That many of the story's elements derive from the author's youth demonstrates its profound importance for him. The taxidermist Philarète, the childhood nurse who became the subject of an unsavory sexual obsession, the aging alchemist, the three judgmental old sisters, and the shadowy, labyrinthine house itself all belong to an idiosyncratic mythology whose origins we can locate in Jean Ray's formative years. These characters and that house reoccur in varied but recognizable forms throughout the author's oeuvre.

The tendrils of this elaborate narrative, this fox's maze, this tangled gorgon's coiffure, extend well beyond the author's mythologized childhood and his other works. *Malpertuis* also exhibits a degree of intertextuality that is extreme even for Jean Ray, regarding whom the critic Jacques Carion wrote that he "pretends to speak of the real and never stops quoting literature."[5] Jean Ray's works often incorporate direct and sometimes lengthy allusions to other authors (especially Dickens and Chaucer), but here he indulges in intertextuality to an extent far beyond his other works. With over two dozen individual epigraphs, numerous internal quotes and allusions, a dedication to two contemporaries (including a substantial quote from one), and an invocation to the entirety of Greek mythology along with major portions of later European folklore, *Malpertuis* is a novel closely woven into the millennia-old fabric of Western literature and oral tradition.

The surprise is that many of these intercalary texts appear to be complete fabrications, even those attributed to such canonical authors as Hawthorne, Voltaire, and Sterne. Whether Jean Ray manufactured these passages himself, paraphrased them, or derived them from extremely loose earlier translations remains difficult to determine. Equally surprising is that previous scholars did not notice this. The exception is Van Herp, who noted that the epigraph about living eyes in jars from "Wickstead's *Grimoire*" was "solely the issue of Jean Ray's pen" (in fact, both Wickstead and his *Grimoire* appear to be Jean Ray's creations).

Thus it seems the old prankster played one more trick, one that has remained almost entirely undiscovered until now, nearly eighty years later. What makes his game more complicated is that *not all* the passages quoted in *Malpertuis* are spurious or misattributed. The Poe quote is legitimate and accurately cited, and the portion of a universal orison from an eighteenth-century Christian prayerbook appears verbatim. So many others, however, must derive either from the author's imagination, his memory, or from old and superseded translations still unavailable online. If Jean Ray meant these interpolations as part of one big joke, he obscured his intentions by blending a handful of legitimate quotations in with his own manufactured examples. Though Iain White may have harbored suspicions of his own regarding some of these passages, he remained moot on the point.

Now that we have reached the approximate center of this afterword, the time seems right to present a small but richly deserved encomium in recognition of Iain White, the excellent translator of *Malpertuis*. Of my half dozen or so predecessors in the translation of Jean Ray's work, White stands out (this is not to take away from the others, especially Lowell Bair, whose English versions of Jean Ray's prose in the 1964 collection *Ghouls in My Grave* were my own introduction to the author's work, and which retain a remarkable freshness and life almost six decades later). Wakefield Press publisher Marc Lowenthal and I both admire White's translation, and we agreed early on that however close a fresh translation might come to matching the quality of his work, it would be difficult to surpass to any significant degree. We should be grateful to Iain White for this fine translation (slightly edited and annotated in this edition, but lacking nothing of his original).

Biographical information on White remains scant, however. Perhaps this absence is the ultimate achievement of the professional translator: to fade like a ghost behind the texts one ferries back across the Styx. Best known for his translations of works from the twentieth-century avant-garde (Dada, surrealism, Oulipo, etc.), Iain White was born in 1929. In his youth he frequented London's Soho/Fitzrovia literary bohemia. In his later life he graduated from Cambridge with a degree in social anthropology. Afterward he went to work for twenty years as a copy editor in academic publishing. Key among his many translations were *The King in the Golden Mask* by Marcel Schwob (Carcanet, 1982; expanded edition Tartarus Press, 2012); *Visits of Love* by Alfred Jarry (Atlas Press, 1993); *The Gangsters* by Hervé Guibert (Serpent's Tail, 1991); *The House of Oracles* by Thomas Owen (Tartarus Press, 2012); and perhaps most importantly, *The Tutu* by Léon Genonceaux (Atlas Press, 2013). His original translation of *Malpertuis* (Atlas Press, 1998) has proven especially enduring. Sources suggest that Iain White died in 2017, but even this remains difficult to verify.

Thanks to Iain White, *Malpertuis* has been available in English for over two decades. Even if the novel has not yet achieved the full prominence in the world's literature that it arguably deserves, the various editions in at least eight languages have brought it some measure of renown. The novel's notable admirers include director Alain Resnais (1922–2014), the director of *Hiroshima Mon Amour* and *Last Year at Marienbad*, and the late Genesis Breyer P-Orridge (1950–2020), lead vocalist of Throbbing Gristle and Psychic TV. Crucially, it also attracted the early attention of authors Raymond Queneau (1903–1976) and Roland Stragliati (1909–1999), leading them to befriend the author and become his champions. Their dedicated efforts led to the return of *Malpertuis* to print in 1956, and ultimately to the revival of Jean Ray's literary career on a scale he had not experienced since the triumphant reception of his debut collection *Whiskey Tales* in the 1920s, along with a permanent place in the canon of Francophone speculative fiction. Although Resnais never achieved his goal of bringing Jean Ray's work to the screen (his interest was in the Harry Dickson detective stories), Belgian director Harry Kümel adapted *Malpertuis* in 1971 into a film starring Orson Welles. Alas, Jean Ray passed away in 1964, so he never saw it.[6]

Kümel's film is beautiful and lush, and although some parts follow the novel very closely, especially those scenes set inside Malpertuis itself, the end and beginning are quite different and alter the overall narrative. The novel has also been the subject of multiple musical and theatrical adaptations, including the 2001 *Tchiek*, an absurd production combining large marionettes with living actors and inspired as much by Tod Browning's *Freaks*, Monty Python's *Life of Brian*, Edgar Allan Poe, and Alfred Jarry as by Jean Ray. This version combines the characters of Tchiek and Jean-Jacques Grandsire.[7]

What has led to the longevity of this peculiar novel, when so many of its contemporaries, including, for instance, the work of Jules Stéphane, to whom Jean Ray dedicated it, have not only fallen out of print but have vanished into obscurity? Perhaps *Malpertuis* might have met a similar fate, along with the rest of Jean Ray's oeuvre, if not for the advocacy of Queneau and Stragliati. Ray's multiple pseudonyms and frequent switching between two languages and various media and genres certainly did not work in his favor. His vast output, however, probably meant that his reputation would at least have seen a posthumous revival had it not gotten a boost during his final decade.

Yet *Malpertuis* is *sui generis*. Quite likely its destiny always included some degree of recognition. Like Isidore Ducasse's *Les Chants de Maldoror*, revived and canonized by the surrealists, its rediscovery may have been inevitable. Here we have a novel almost entirely postmodern in structure by an author who altogether eschewed modernism, postmodernism, and any form of avant-garde literature. The elaborate composition of *Malpertuis*, with its multiple perspectives and shifting realities, constructed in the manner of Russian *matryoshka* dolls, carries the gothic into the postmodern without ever passing through the intermediary steps.

Jean Ray's vehicle for this transfer, which largely precedes the arrival of postmodernism proper, seems to be post-Newtonian physics. Though not as explicitly developed a theme as in some of his other key works, Ray nonetheless makes this clear when he allows the Abbé Doucedame to describe the tale's titular manse as "a kind of 'fold in space,' to explain the juxtaposition of two worlds, different in essence, between which Malpertuis might be considered an abominable point of contact." Of course, many other writers had also tapped into the ideas of Einstein, Planck, and Bohr by 1943. Few of them managed to produce successful novels, however. Here, perhaps, we find the full measure of *Malpertuis*: though not fully weird, it is nonetheless filled with cosmic dread. With the primary exception of the novels of the British author William Hope Hodgson (1877–1918), few other writers managed to accomplish such an atmosphere at this length prior to the current century.

This device allows Ray to position Cassave's mansion as a nexus of all things unwholesome and otherworldly, a place where ancient entities persist in strange forms and eternity bleeds into the present. By choosing the name of the house as the name of the book, the novel takes on this property as well. This draws directly on the ancient meaning of the name: for Reynard the fox, Malpertuis was a house with many exits, many escape routes. Ray's Malpertuis, as Jean-Jacques Grandsire and others discover, is a place all too easy to find, but much more difficult to escape. Critic François Angelier recently pointed out how the descriptions of the décor of Malpertuis, which combines both Christian and pagan symbols, and its architecture, which remains elusive overall despite many specific details, make it difficult to situate in time and space and impossible to map internally.[8] Malpertuis thus joins every great haunted house in literature before and since, from the Castle of Otranto, to Hill House and the House of Leaves, while simultaneously retaining its own fantastic identity.

Another aspect of *Malpertuis* deserves our attention as well. Where another author might have offered us only one of the taxidermied Olympians, or the stipulations of Cassave's will and the scenario it creates, or the werewolf subplot centered around poor doomed Abbé Doucedame, Ray does not hold back. Devices that for some writers might have served as the focus of an entire novel become almost throwaways in this one. His creative largesse makes the novel's multiple nested manuscripts and narratives seem almost necessities. These mechanisms allow Ray to parcel out his array of tricks in digestible doses and more than justify the repeat readings that have become a feature for so many readers. The novel also ties into much of his other work, though more by way of motifs and themes than in the more obvious shared settings of Faulkner, Lovecraft, and Stephen King. Finally, in the narrative's outer frame, we find the thief of Jean Ray's ultimate metafiction: the shady protagonist of his manufactured autobiography.

Malpertuis, then, is a labyrinth of words set in a labyrinthine mansion. It is not a minotaur that lurks at its heart, though; for *Malpertuis* is ultimately a love story, or at least the story of a tragic love triangle. As it is a tragedy, Jean-Jacques does not inherit Cassave's mansion and fortune. The novel's final sentences reveal the ultimate beneficiary of the ancient alchemist's legacy, Medusa's immortal sister Euryale. Jean Ray invites us to feel the pathos of one of Western civilization's best-known monsters.

As the first half of *Malpertuis* opens with successive narrative levels that each build suspense and dread, each level of the second half closes with tragedy and horror. Mathias Krook, Lampernisse, Nancy, Abbé Doucedame, and finally Jean-Jacques Grandsire himself all meet their terrible fates, to the increasing refrain of "*Moïra, Moïra . . .*"[9] But the revelation of the final tragedy comes from the nameless thief who began the narrative: it is not the doom of Jean-Jacques Grandsire, turned to stone in an instant, but the dreadful fate of the immortal Euryale, the last of the three Gorgon sisters, doomed to wander the empty corridors of Malpertuis alone for all eternity: "a creature of great beauty—but terrible as God . . . weeping great moonlight-colored tears."[10]

This denouement asks us to consider the curse of immortality, and of the deities of Western civilization's pagan roots lingering overlong into the Christian era. We see here also the unique admixture of Jean Ray's fiction: a world where pagan deities, *outré* modern physics, and the complete and very literal pantheon of Belgian Catholicism all have their places. Though Euryale may be a monster, and her final appearance in the novel invokes terror, we are meant to pity her nonetheless. The thief escapes with his life—barely—but the Gorgon remains trapped forever, her prison the site of a drama long played out, her last chance at love lost. Malpertuis, old Reynard's ancient warren of escape passages, has become a dungeon for Euryale. As long as this novel remains in print, she will walk the halls of her otherwise-deserted mansion, weeping her lunar tears, with no sympathetic deity to hear her prayers. It is a bleak note on which to end, tempered only slightly by the thief's escape to tell us the tale.

Malpertuis the novel mirrors Malpertuis the house: an edifice of interconnected passageways, some with no clear end, inhabited by gods,

EDITOR'S AFTERWORD

demigods, furies, gorgons, and even a much-diminished titan. This condensed complexity is one of the book's strengths, and Ray's elaborate game of intertextual references opens its own set of doorways to other times. I have drawn the reader's particular attention to the matter of this volume's abundant epigraphs because these short texts play their own special role in the book's structure. The deliberate nature of this role becomes obvious upon the recognition that Jean Ray penned many of them himself (and even created some of the authors and/or volumes). In a work of obvious fiction ostensibly presented as truth via the old device of found manuscripts (a device the reader may appreciate but is unlikely to accept as altogether realistic), Jean Ray also threads his text with lardons of fiction that masquerade as truth. The obvious layers of the novel disguise the questionable nature of the very epigraphs that announce them. Though he may not have been the real-life pirate that he painted himself out to be, this discovery shows that he was every bit the literary rogue.

Malpertuis begins and ends with the words of a master thief, ostensibly that fictional persona from the author's own fictional biography. Does he not imply here that this narrator is intended to be read as "Jean Ray" when he writes "I am obliged to add my own name to the roll of those scribes who, without their knowledge (or almost without it), have given Malpertuis a place in the history of human terror"? No other name appears in the text to identify the thief. In addition to that long roll of scribes (some fictional), the narrator/author, the dreadful mansion, and the mysterious White Fathers, the novel's frame also includes the Hellenic supernaturals, though by the outer edge of that frame, they have suffered a grievous attrition and diminishment, such that only Medusa's obscure but immortal sister retains her full divinity. Ultimately in *Malpertuis*, this onion of many layers, Jean Ray asks us to shed one last tear when we reach its denouement: sympathy for the last lonely gorgon.

ACKNOWLEDGMENTS

André Verbrugghen has continued to provide indispensable information on the most esoteric corners of *le monde Rayen*. For this volume, he also enlisted to our aid several other members of of L'Amicale Jean Ray, including Michel Barran, Johnny Bekaert, Hervé Louinet, Patrick Mecucci, and Bart Bruggeman, who resolved the mystery of *la canemuche*, that peculiar *hapax legomenon* of the Jean Ray oeuvre. International scholar Svyatoslav Albeiro, who is translating some of my own work into Russian, helped me to tackle the mystery of Jean Ray's questionable epigraphs. Author Anya Martin continues to copyedit every word I write, always making things better, never worse. All readers of Jean Ray should share my gratitude to Marc Lowenthal and Wakefield Press for continuing to make this project a reality.

Sadly, author, editor, and publisher Jean Pelan, who started me on my journey with Jean Ray several decades ago, passed away during the final preparation of this volume, so he will not get to see it. I am grateful that he *was* able to enjoy the previous four volumes of Jean Ray's work in English from Wakefield Press. John was a longtime Jean Ray booster in the Anglophone world, and the *primum mobile* of this project. His memory and his enthusiasm for making this important author available to a wider readership will continue to guide it.

Scott Nicolay

NOTES

1. Arnaud Huftier, "Postface," in *Malpertuis: Histoire d'Une Maison Fantastique,* by Jean Ray (Paris: Alma, 2017). Huftier's massive *Jean Ray, l'alchimie du mystère* (Paris: Les Belles Lettres, 2010) remains the essential bibliographic reference for all Jean Ray scholarship.

2. Jean Ray, "Aux Lisières des Ténèbres," in *Cahiers de L'Herne: Jean Ray*, ed. Jacques Van Herp and François Truchaud (Paris: Éditions de L'Herne, 1981), 158–184.

3. Geert Vandamme, *Soms overtreft de werkelijkheid de fantasie: Raymond De Kremer, Alias Jean Ray/John Flanders 1887–1964: Een biografie*, 2 vols. (Gent: Poespa, 2019).

4. I discuss the interrelationships between these texts at greater length in "Of Haunted Books and Intercalary Ghosts," the afterword to *The Great Nocturnal* (Cambridge, MA: Wakefield Press, 2020), 103–119.

5. Jacques Carion, "Jean Ray feint de parler du réel et n'arrête pas de citer la littérature," in *Jean Ray: Un Livre, Une Oeuvre* (Brussels: Editions Labor, 1986).

6. Jean Ray died just five weeks before the opening of *Le Grande Frousse* (*The Great Fright*), French director Jean-Pierre Mocky's 1964 film adaptation of *La Cité de l'Indicible Peur* (*The City of Unspeakable Fear*). This mosaic novel, forthcoming in English translation from Wakefield Press, was Jean Ray's next book after *Malpertuis*.

7. "Tcheik," https://www.froefroe.be/en/production/974/tchiek, accessed 8 May 2021.

8. François Angelier, "Malpertuis ou les dieux en exil," *Bifrost 87 Jean Ray: Peur Sur la Ville* (2017): 142–146.

9. Lampernisse reveals his true identity with his final words, via a mostly untranslatable pun (*Promettez/Prométhée*), which has been rendered in this edition as "Promise me this"/Prometheus.

10. Not surprisingly, it took Sophie Théry, one of the few female scholars of Jean Ray's work, to point out that the Gorgon is both the central and the final signifier in the novel. See Sophie Théry, "La Gnose dans Malpertuis," in *Otrante no. 4, Art et Littérature Fantastiques: Jean Ray/John Flanders Croisement d'Ombres* (Paris: Editions Kimé, 2003), 133–145.

Iain White (1929–2017) was the translator of, among others, Marcel Schwob, Alfred Jarry, Hervé Guibert, Thomas Owen, Léon Genonceaux, Georges Limbour, Benjamin Péret, and Jean Ray.

Archaeologist, caver, father, educator, podcaster, activist, translator, DJ, World Fantasy Award–winner, Scott Nicolay has been many things. But never a minister.

THE SCHOOL OF THE STRANGE